SIREN
Publishing

Ménage Everlasting

# The Shadow's Leap

Marla Monroe

Mates of the Jaguar 1

Mates of the Jaguar 1

# The Shadow's Leap

Taylor isn't ready for a mate, but then she finds herself with two that she doesn't know what to do with. They are adamant that she is theirs, even when her leader says she is to mate with the jaguars' leader instead. Can she defy her uncle at the expense of her Leap? If she refuses her uncle's bidding, another leader my take over her Leap and kill all of the males. If she agrees, she loses her true mates.

Marco and Rubio have waited years for their true mate and don't plan on losing her once they find her. They appeal to their leader to allow them to claim their mate. In doing so, they could be condemning their shadow to living in the jungle with a drug cartel using them to do its dirty work.

If there is a third option, can they agree to take it? Will Taylor risk her Leap in order to claim her mates?

**Genre:** Contemporary, Ménage a Trois/Quatre, Paranormal, Shape-shifter
**Length:** 30,012 words

# THE SHADOW'S LEAP

## *Mates of the Jaguar 1*

### Marla Monroe

Siren Publishing, Inc.
www.SirenPublishing.com

A SIREN PUBLISHING BOOK

THE SHADOW'S LEAP
Copyright © 2017 by Marla Monroe

ISBN: 978-1-64010-886-8

First Publication: November 2017

Cover design by Harris Channing
All art and logo copyright © 2017 by Siren Publishing, Inc.

**ALL RIGHTS RESERVED:** This literary work may not be reproduced or transmitted in any form or by any means, including electronic or photographic reproduction, in whole or in part, without express written permission.

All characters and events in this book are fictitious. Any resemblance to actual persons living or dead is strictly coincidental.

WARNING: The unauthorized reproduction or distribution of this copyrighted work is illegal. Criminal copyright infringement, including infringement without monetary gain, is investigated by the FBI and is punishable by up to 5 years in federal prison and a fine of $250,000.

If you find a Siren-BookStrand e-book or print book being sold or shared illegally, please let us know at
**legal@sirenbookstrand.com**

**PUBLISHER**
Siren Publishing, Inc.
www.SirenPublishing.com

# ABOUT THE AUTHOR

Marla Monroe has been writing professionally for nearly thirteen years. Her first book with Siren was published in January 2011, and she now has over 75 books available with them. She loves to write and spends every spare minute either at the keyboard or reading. She writes everything from sizzling-hot cowboys, emotionally charged BDSM, and dangerously addictive shifters to science fiction ménages with the occasional badass biker thrown in for good measure.

Marla lives in the southern US and works full-time at a busy hospital. When not writing, she loves to travel, spend time with her feline muses, and read. Although she misses her cross-stitch and putting together puzzles, she is much happier writing fantasy worlds where she can make everyone's dreams come true. She's always eager to try something new and thoroughly enjoys the research she does for her books. She loves to hear from readers about what they are looking for in their reading adventures.

*E-mail:*
themarlamonroe@yahoo.com

*Website:*
www.marlamonroe.com

*Blog:*
www.themarlamonroe.blogspot.com

*Twitter:*
@MarlaMonroe1

*Facebook:*
www.facebook.com/marla.monroe.7

*Google+:*
www.plus.google.com/u/0/+marlamonroe7/posts

*Goodreads:*
www.goodreads.com/author/show/4562866.Marla_Monroe

*Pinterest:*
www.pinterest.com/marlamonroe

*Amazon:*
www.amzn.to/1euRooO

**For all titles by Marla Monroe, please visit**
www.bookstrand.com/marla-monroe

# THE SHADOW'S LEAP

*Mates of the Jaguar 1*

MARLA MONROE
Copyright © 2017

## Chapter One

"Damn them!" Marco snatched up the small limp body of a human child and ran with him toward home. "Grab the other one, Rubio. Diaz and Miguel are covering us."

Marco watched as his twin scooped the child lying crumpled on the ground into his arms. The poor thing had been lying less than five feet from her mother's butchered body. His brother would have no way to know if the child was alive or not until they reached their home. At least they wouldn't end up as some scavenger's next meal.

As soon as they reached the outskirts of their community, Marco slowed down and adjusted the child in his arms to a more comfortable position. It was possible he was doing more harm to the young boy with how he'd carried him away from the fighting. He prayed that he hadn't.

Rubio swung open the gate to their back veranda where they often watched the shadow's young. Several pallets of soft grasses lay scattered near the house beneath the shade of the awning for when one of the young needed to rest.

He and his brother gently laid the two human children on the pallets. Both were covered in blood, but Marco hoped it was the children's madre and not theirs.

"The female is breathing, brother, but she has a serious cut on her arm. It's almost to the bone. I'll be right back." Rubio ran into the house.

Marco knew he would bring back supplies to tend to the children. The little male child he'd managed to save didn't seem to have any cuts but had a nasty bump on his head where someone had hit him with something heavy. He prayed there would be no brain injury or swelling. They were well over an hour from the nearest hospital. In the wilds of the Central American jungle where they lived, the law of the jungle still lived on. Only the strong survived, and when someone was injured, more than likely they would die. Marco didn't want that for these young.

His Shadow, the name for a jaguar family or group, lived deep in the rain forest where they had thrived for many hundreds of years. That was before the deforestation and the influx of cartels, drug lords, and the crooked military. Now innocents were slaughtered when his Shadow refused to do their dirty work.

"Here, brother." Rubio handed Marco the box of medical supplies. "How is the little male child?"

"He has a cut and a large knot on his forehead, but I don't see any other cuts on his body. Head wounds bleed a lot, and some of the blood on him is probably his madre's, as well." Marco used some gauze and saline to begin cleaning the blood and dirt from the male child as Rubio did the same for the little female.

"She needs stitches in this arm. We need to take them to our healer. We can't care for them here, and I want back out to fight those bastards. I don't think I can take much more of this carnage, brother."

"Neither can I. We'll leave them with the healer and return to help transport the injured into Suchitito once the fighting is over. I want the blood of the one who cut down the females. He used a machete, so he should be easy to find." Marco finished cleaning the young male's wound before picking him up and carrying him close to his chest as if he were spun glass. His brother did the same with his bundle.

He followed Rubio to the hut where their healer, Carlos, lived. He was a good deal older than they were but still moved as easily as one half his age. The healer met them at the door when Rubio called out from a few yards away.

"What are you bringing me?" He looked down at their burdens. "Put them over there."

They settled the young on a soft bed in the back of the main room of Carlos's home. He immediately began checking them over.

"The bastards are warning us again that if we won't fight for them they will continue to kill the innocents in front of us. They killed their mother and nearly got them before we arrived and attacked them." Marco pulled the soft blanket away from the male child's face and head. "He doesn't have any other injuries that I could find except his head. He's been unconscious since I picked him up."

"Hmm." Carlos looked him over then moved to the female child. "And what have we here?"

"They nearly cut her arm in two. I've wrapped it, but it needs stitches and a good cleaning." Rubio unwrapped the bandage so that Carlos could see.

"Pigs! To do this to children. They should be drawn and quartered." Carlos had little patience with those who harmed females and their young.

"We agree. Do you need our help? We'd like to return to fight with the others." Marco waited for the healer's nod.

"Go and wipe them out. I can care for these two young. I'll call for Maria to help once they wake. Hurry before the fighting is over and you get no revenge in their madre's name."

They nodded and stripped as they left, shifting to their jaguars on the run. It wasn't as fluid or painless as when they had time to flow into their cats, but they didn't want to take the time. Once they rid their territory of this group of drug lords another would soon pop up, but what choice did they have?

Jag, the Felix of their Shadow, had talked about taking over the entire territory and killing anyone who attempted to start up another drug business in it, but that would require more males and more effort to keep the area free of the bastards. Plus, it would put their females and young in greater danger than they were already in.

As soon as they reached the edge of the fighting, Marco felt a bullet whiz past his ear. This was new. They rarely fought with guns when engaging them. They didn't want to kill them. The cartels needed them as muscle for their operations. Another bullet grazed his shoulder. Rage burned with the adrenaline pumping through his bloodstream now. He charged the bastard with the gun and took him down in one leap.

*One down, but I still need to find the one with the machete if the others haven't already gotten to him. The young deserve justice for the loss of their madre.*

Marco looked up to see Rubio stretched out on a limb in a tree, his focus on a male with two knives as he chased a young human male of about fifteen or so years. His brother let the young male pass then sprang from the branch to take out the *bastardo* as he passed beneath the limb. Marco didn't need to stick around to see if his brother killed him or not. That was a given. He needed to find the one responsible for the mutilation of that poor female and her young child.

A loud guttural scream cut short from behind him only verified what Marco had already known. Rubio didn't miss. Marco swiped at a human carrying a large knife, but it wasn't the one he wanted. The dirty male went down without even seeing what hit him.

He continued chasing after one human piece of trash after another then, finally, just a few hundred yards away, stood his target. He had a female by her hair with the machete at her throat. He was yelling at Jag and Diaz that unless they agreed to patrol their drug warehouses to keep anyone from stealing their merchandise, he would slash her neck so that she bled out slow.

"She'll die a painful death if you don't agree to my terms, animal." His stilted English was nearly impossible to understand. Why he spoke in English and not Spanish, Marco had no idea.

The bastard lowered the blade and made a quick small cut to the woman's chest just above her heaving breasts. He heard her indrawn breath, but she didn't whimper or cry out. He respected her strength and vowed he'd do what he could to save her.

While Jag and Diaz tried to negotiate with him, Marco circled around behind the man, using the fighting going on around him to mask his approach. He knew the moment Diaz spotted him. He didn't let on, but the quick shift of the male's right hand was all he needed to know that they would provide an opportunity for him to strike.

All it would take was one quick bite to the man's skull and he'd crush it, stopping all movement from the bastard so he wouldn't slash the female's throat as he fell. He'd aim for the part just above the cervical spine. It would give the female the best chance of escaping without injury.

Marco froze not ten feet from the male human and his prisoner. Jag threw up his hands and yelled, "Fine! You win. Release her and you have our word we will fight for you as long as you are in charge."

Marco had to fight to keep from chuffing in amusement at Jag's play on words. If he had his say, the male's days of being in charge were limited to the next ten seconds or less.

"*Espléndido!*" He dropped his arm and took a step back but then swung the knife in an arc that would decapitate the poor female's head if he didn't manage to catch the man's arm instead of his neck.

Marco leapt, managed to grab the male's arm, and snapped it clean off, stopping the machete from digging into the female's neck. Instead, the male screamed, running around with most of his arm missing. Marco left the female to Jag and Diaz. He had wounded prey to chase down. It didn't take long. The idiot hadn't stopped the blood flow, which would have been the smart thing to do. Instead he'd run around pumping it out faster until he'd collapsed at the base of a tree.

Standing over him, Marco's brother dripped saliva from his fangs onto the dying man's face. The big cat opened his mouth wide and growled. The low guttural sound, along with a loud hiss, would even frighten other large cats. If possible, the man grew even paler.

While Rubio terrorized the human piece of filth, Marco walked over him to sit next to the human filth and took a nice long lick of the adrenaline-laced blood from what was left of his arm then smacked his lips and cleaned his muzzle with his tongue. That and his brother staring down at him with a mouth full of teeth were the last things he saw before he died.

Marco stared at his brother and nodded. They'd done it. Not only had they avenged the poor humans but they'd wiped out an entire cartel. Unfortunately, they both knew that another one would fill the empty void within a week or two. Their only recourse was to either take over the territory or move.

Their Felix was trying to find somewhere in the United States to settle where they wouldn't have war lords or cartels trying to bully them into being their muscle. Finding territory was proving to be more difficult than Jag had first believed. Most of the shifters in the US didn't want a shadow of jaguars anywhere near their door.

He and his brother had no idea how everything would turn out, but they did know that something had to change and soon. He, along with many other males, was slowly going insane watching the carnage over and over again. That the humans hadn't yet targeted their females and young was the only thing that kept the jaguars from eliminating any human male they encountered. It was just a matter of time though. Eventually they would take that step and damn them all to hell.

"We've stopped this one, brother." Rubio had changed and was attempting to wipe some of the blood off of him with a large leaf he'd picked up from the ground.

Marco remained in his jaguar form. He didn't want to be human for a while longer. Though his human side didn't do such atrocious things, he needed to be free of him for a little longer.

Instead, he chuffed at his brother to let him know that he agreed. Rubio steered away from their community toward one of the tributaries of the river where he could wash off before returning home. Neither one of them wanted to carry any part of the carnage into their home. It was a sanctuary for them. One that they hoped to someday bring their mate to live.

"Come on, Marco. Time to get this crap off of us. I can't stand the stench of it."

Marco dove in ahead of his brother and swam around beneath the water before coming up for air. Rubio had dived in right behind him and was even now treading water while he rubbed at his hair to clean the blood from it. It was too bad that when they shifted back to their human side the blood didn't disappear. Instead it coated their bare skin.

"How long do you think before the next one shows up?" Rubio wasn't looking at him now. He still concentrated on cleaning his long hair.

Marco sighed and allowed the change to flow through him. In the water it was a little more difficult as he sank before he was able to function, but when he broke the surface again, he still didn't have an answer.

"Not long enough, brother. Not long enough."

# Chapter Two

"What do you think?" Marco leaned back against the wide Kapok tree, lifting his arms up the tree's trunk in a satisfying stretch before relaxing back into a comfortable slump.

"I wish we could settle in Louisiana. Florida would be okay, but I prefer the wilder areas in the swamps." Rubio tugged on the clouded leopard's scruff then rolled the cat over to rub her belly. "I'm fucking tired of watching them parade women and children in front of us as reminders that they'll slaughter them if we don't play their games."

"They aren't going to stop." Marco pushed away from the tree with one bare foot to join his twin brother wrestling with the leopard cub on the jungle floor. "If we stay, the humans here will never be safe, and eventually, neither will our females and cubs." He yanked the growling cub's tail as she popped at Rubio's hand then back at his.

"There aren't many choices, though. Jag and Diaz are trying to negotiate some land in both places, but so far they haven't made much headway." Rubio shook his head. "Here, the government doesn't care that we're shifters. They view us as a step above the low-life fuckers who fight among themselves. In the States, our kind is acknowledged yet closely supervised. They're smart enough to fear us but ignorant enough to let us govern ourselves."

"That can be a blessing for us, Rubio. We'll have some rights where here we have nothing. They kill our kind if they see an opportunity. There, it is illegal to kill a shifter."

"But they are always watching the shifters. I am afraid I'll feel like a bug under a microscope." Rubio sighed and stroked the cub's fur.

Marco tended to agree with his brother. The idea of someone always watching and taking notes bothered him. Still, that was preferable to what they had here. The promise of peace, or as much as you can have among shifter groups, seemed like a dream to him.

The only other downside to living Stateside would be the politics. Even though Jag and Diaz would handle the majority of it, depending on what they did once they moved, he and his brother would have to deal with some of it, as well. His brother was content to trust their shadow's leaders to pick their way through the bullshit ceremonies of shifter politics, but that would change.

He also wondered how other groups would view their open policy of allowing other cat shifters into their shadow. The majority of their members were jaguars, but over the years, before shifters made themselves known to humans, feline shifter numbers had dwindled, where the canine and lupine had risen. No one knew the reason despite scores of dollars in research, but because of the decrease, their Felix had agreed to allow other feline species into their shadow.

With the new influx of blood, their numbers grew, albeit slowly, yet still they increased. Now Marco and Rubio often found themselves entertaining a cub or two at their place. So far, neither of them had produced a cub of their own, but neither had they been spreading their seed around in order for that to happen. Both wanted to find their true mate, despite that not happening in many years among their shadow.

Many shifter groups were purists in that they didn't allow or condone cross breading. That led to a compromised gene pool and inbreeding. Their healer believed it was why so many of the cat shifter groups had few cubs born. The canine and lupine groups had no such issues. There were far more of them than the cats. The canines seemed to breed with any shifter group, and though the lupines were more selective, they, too, allowed other groups outside of cats into their packs.

Jag, their shadow's Felix, had handled negotiations between shifter groups and between their shadow and the human cartels for years. The pressures seemed to increase daily until he couldn't keep up with everything on his own. His personal assistant, Diaz, helped with some of the more mundane issues, but anything requiring decisions or negotiation remained on the Felix's shoulders. It didn't help matters that he had a nasty temper, which often put a halt to all negotiations.

With their world narrowing down on them, Jag had been wise enough to realize that he needed someone who could dance the dance without getting backed into a corner and under the mercy of another group and still remain cool.

Diaz's role changed from glorified personal assistant to one of liaison to other shifter groups and the local government. He held the title of Second and Shadow Counsel. Marco knew it had been a wise move on Jag's part to admit his weakness and move to shore that weakness up by utilizing one of their own. The move had already proved to be a wise decision on the part of their Felix.

"I don't think we're going to be accepted in either place." Rubio picked up the now sleeping cub and carried her over to the soft bed of grasses and wild orchids he'd made for the various cubs who often spent time with them when their *madres* needed to be gone for a while.

"I'm worried that you're right. Both feline groups are much smaller than we are since we have allowed so many other felines into our shadow. They're intimidated by our size and the fact that we're mostly made up of jaguars." Marco sighed and watched the sleeping cub breathe in and out, oblivious of the cruel, shrinking world around her.

"I'm not sure where that leaves us. Many of the states are made up of either deserts or months of snow and ice. While I'm not averse to the occasional cold winter, I'm not a fan of extended snowy seasons." Rubio clasped his hands behind his head.

"I'm worried he may decide to accept the tentative offer from the cougar pard in the northeast." Marco sighed and rubbed his chin. "I believe the New England states are where they are. The winters there are brutal."

"So we either face ice and snow for months on end or continue as we are, under the thumb of drug lords who enjoy causing misery. I don't see that we've got many options, brother. If my vote counted, I'd say we remain here and actively protect the humans in our territory and push the cartels out once and for all." Rubio drew in a deep breath and let it out in a soft whoosh. "That won't happen, and our options are dwindling, what few we have, while we wait."

"It all takes time, Rubio. It all takes time." Marco looked down at the sleeping cub as she dreamed her way through sleep, no doubt chasing bugs or maybe even a butterfly. Her little paws raced in sleep even as soft mewling snarls tickled the air. "I just hope it doesn't take so much time that the shadow's cubs join the humans in constant danger."

\* \* \* \*

Taylor Dristal stared out the window of the twin-engine plane praying they made it to the landing strip. Hell, she prayed the pilot knew where the damn thing was, hidden away in the dense foliage below them. She'd had little desire to visit the Central American countries, and if she'd realized what her Felix had in store for her, she might have pretended to be sick with menstrual cramps, anything to escape flying on a wind-up toy plane into a jungle she doubted she could survive alone despite being a leopard shifter.

*Why me? He could have sent Toni or even Gayle who kept the Leap's records. I had to have done something to piss him off but just can't think of what it was.*

She had no idea what to expect from a jaguar shadow who was looking to relocate and hadn't fared well in negotiations with the Louisiana pard or the panthers in the Florida glades. More than likely they would be snarling cats who'd just as soon snap her neck as listen to her absurd offer from her Felix. Taylor still wasn't sure how she felt about the offer he'd trusted her with in the first place.

Darrius, their Felix, was close to seventy years old. He'd lost two mates and worried that he'd waited too long and was now too weak to keep their Leap safe anymore. The problem was that there wasn't anyone else in their shifter community strong enough to take over. Taylor could agree with that, but offering their Leap to a strange shifter group seemed more like suicide than a solid decision.

"I can't believe I'm doing this. I should have tried to talk him out of it." But Taylor knew there would have been no talking the old cat out of anything he thought was in the best interest of his family.

Stepping back, she understood the need and even why he didn't petition other feline groups to interview potential replacements. One or more of them would decide to take matters into their own hands and demand a leadership match. Just because they were able to best Darrius didn't mean they should be the Leap's Felix. Leadership matches were to the death, and the winner automatically assumed the role of Felix.

Taylor shuddered to think of some of the potential leaders who'd picked up on Darrius' weakening state and camped out close by to watch for an opportunity to take over. The Leap had closed ranks around their Felix, knowing he was trying to find them a strong, understanding one to replace him.

"Make sure you're buckled up tight back there and secure anything you're working on. We're about to land, and the descent is going to be sharp since we only have a small window of visibility to the landing strip." The pilot's matter-of-fact attitude did little to reassure her as the plane took a sudden dip that felt like a free fall at first.

*I swear if I live through this crap I'm going to demand that Darrius takes me off the ambassador list. It was only supposed to be for a year in the first place. I should have already rotated off. Lying bastard.*

Another sharp dive and Taylor slammed her eyes shut, squeezing them so tightly stars danced behind her eyelids. The sudden loss of altitude had her stomach in her throat and her last meal fast approaching the release valve. Finally, they leveled out, and seconds later, the jarring of the plane bouncing on the tarmac gave her some measure of relief.

"Piece of cake, Cap. Piece of cake. Told you I could handle it."

Realization that the actual pilot hadn't landed the plane redoubled her resolve of refusing to do this type of work ever again.

"Miss Dristal? You can open your eyes now. We're ready to depart. Your luggage will be sent directly to your hostel."

Taylor immediately recognized the voice as belonging to the one who'd evidently landed the plane. She opened her eyes to see the flight steward standing over her with her computer bag ready for her departure.

*No freaking way am I getting on another plane with him. He doesn't look old enough to vote, much less pilot a plane. I'll kill Darrius for this.*

"Careful going down the ramp, now. It can be slick in this humidity."

Taylor took the proffered computer bag and carefully walked down the ramp, holding on to one rail as she did. The last thing she needed was some sort of injury that would delay her return home.

Humid air hit her like a force field, taking her breath almost as soon as she stepped off the plane. It only got worse as she walked down the ramp. Already her blouse clung to her body, and her short hair felt unruly when she ran her fingers through it. Taylor groaned. She already had a difficult time controlling the wild curls. As long as she was in Central America she would have to suffer the mess that probably resembled a bird's nest resting on top of her head.

"Just one more thing to add to my list of complaints. Not that it will do me any good." Taylor repositioned the shoulder strap to the computer bag and followed the dark-skinned man, who was only a couple of inches taller than herself, when he waved her forward.

The fifty or so yards from the plane to the building, which she assumed was the airport office, felt more like a hundred miles. Her lungs felt like a sponge full of water. How could anyone survive in these conditions? That they were overwhelming was an understatement, but then she supposed they were used to it by now.

"Miss Dristal." The good-looking male jaguar standing before her oozed sex appeal as well as the standard arrogance of most feline shifter males.

"And you would be?"

Taylor had quickly learned as an ambassador to never assume anything. For all she knew, the male standing before her could be the Felix of their shadow or a glorified gopher. It always proved wise to know the cats you met, as well as the ones who held positions but were never introduced to you.

"I'm Haze. I assist our Felix with all forms of transportation and scheduling. His second was unable to meet you himself but will meet us at the Felix's home." The handsome male's arm fanned out to indicate that she was to precede him to the opposite door, where another male shifter waited to open it for her.

The ride from the airport to the Felix's home took a good twenty minutes. The cool air conditioning in the car gave her a bit of a chill, but she much preferred that over the smoldering heat outside. The beauty of the jungle as they drove deeper into the trees seemed almost surreal. She'd seen parts of the rain forest on TV but never in person. If it weren't for the intense humidity and severe temperatures, Taylor thought she could easily fall in love with the place.

They were met at the door of the impressive home by a male who made her sex throb from just one look of those rich black eyes. They walked up and down her body before a slow growl escaped from his throat then it abruptly cut off. Taylor resisted the urge, no, the need to wrap herself around the man and put her mark on his neck. She'd never had such a reaction before. It took precedence over everything else, including the all-important meeting with the shadow's Felix.

The male's tall, sleek body spoke of strength and power. His midnight-black hair gleamed beneath the lights of the entrance hall, and his wild scent nearly drove her to her knees. The musky, rich smell, which reminded her of the forest at home just after one of their frequent rainstorms, teased her cat.

*Please let him be just for me. I would love to sample his prowess to see if he can satisfy my leopard. Oh hell. Where did that thought come from?*

Taylor didn't have time for romps of any kind, no matter how tempting the specimen. She also couldn't sample a male who might never step foot on US soil. It would be irritating to only get one taste of one such as this cat who was sure to be amazing. There would only be the one chance unless…

"Our Felix is waiting for you." The deep guttural voice just to the side of the object of her raging hormones startled her. How long had she been staring at the feline god in front of her that she would have missed the second male walking up next to him?

"Of course." Sheesh, was that her voice or a Looney Tunes character's?

Taylor tore her protesting gaze from the man who had to have taken a bath in catnip to focus on the other male in the entrance hall. Though he was just as handsome as the one who still had her leopard's complete attention, there was no interest from her cat. Nor did his scent appeal to her. Yes, the pheromones wafting off his skin gave her goosebumps, but beyond that, she felt nothing for this male. Sex appeal maybe, but not enough to think about rolling in his scent.

"I'm Diaz, the Felix's second." The jaguar bowed slightly at the waist. "It's a pleasure to meet you, Miss Dristal. We greatly appreciate that you've come all this way to see us. It wasn't possible for Sir and I to make a trip to the States at this time." The male jaguar led her down a short hall then indicated a left turn.

At the end of that hall, closed double doors cut from solid mahogany stood as silent sentries against all intruders. The rich, dark, almost maroon color blended well with the shadowy hall. If it hadn't been for her feline sight, Taylor might have missed the intricate carving cut into the doors. An amazingly textured depiction of what could only be a jaguar as it lay next to a smooth, flowing stream demanded appreciation with an arrogant snarl barely noticeable at first. The mighty cat's eyes seemed to look all the way inside her inner-most private thoughts and see all of her secrets. Taylor shook her head to dispel the feeling.

Diaz stepped in front of her to rap once on the door before opening it to reveal a simple yet elegant room beyond the magnificent emblem that Taylor was sure held a threat, or maybe threat was too crass of a word. Maybe promise better described the intense gaze of the carved feline.

Bookshelves lined the walls on either side of the room. At the back of the room, a set of elegant French doors opened out to an impressive deck. The French doors were also mahogany with etched glass allowing a view of the outside. In the middle of the room, a large no-nonsense desk complemented the powerful male sitting behind it.

Not a hair looked out of place as the shadow's Felix watched her enter his lair. To her surprise, he rose and extended his hand to her.

"Miss Dristal, it's a pleasure to meet you. I'm Jag, Felix to this shadow" His deep, sultry voice edged with a thick Latin accent proved difficult to understand at first.

Were all the males in their Shadow this damn sexy? She could sense the eyes of the others slip up and down her back, only to focus on her ass. She had to resist the urge to squirm and, no doubt, raise their interest even higher. Their pheromones filled the air with a musty, enticing scent created to draw a female closer to them. It was working much too well. Taylor's body swayed to the lure.

"Enough!" The Felix's deep voice snapped her out of the haze all of those male hormones had buried her under. "She is not a female to be trifled with. She is our guest and the ambassador to the Felix in Seattle."

Taylor didn't bother to turn around to see which of the felines grumbled under their breath. No doubt they both did.

"Please have a seat, Miss Dristal. Ignore them. It would seem they've lost their civility where you're concerned." The Felix nodded then settled back into his own chair once she'd taken her seat.

"It's Taylor, Sire, and I'm not easily disturbed. We're sexual creatures, or I'd be embarrassed by my reactions." Taylor slowly allowed her body to relax into the comfort of the chair.

She was sure many a feline had succumbed to the relaxing texture of the expensive leather and let down their guard in front of this charismatic Felix. Taylor vowed not to become another victim while she was there presenting her Felix's request and subsequent offer of their Leap.

She was also supposed to form an impression of the shadow's Felix to be sure he was, as presented, the strong but fair Felix they'd been led to believe. If not, she was to offer only a safe plot of territory if no other feline group did.

"When your Felix asked if you could come to present an alternative to our relocation to the New England states, I admit I was intrigued. Perhaps you can tell me what this alternative might entail." The Felix leaned back in his chair with one hand on the boot of the leg he'd effortlessly crossed and the other behind his head as he rested it against the chair's high back.

Taylor fought the need to clear her throat. She refused to exhibit nerves, despite knowing they could smell it drifting in the air around her. The sooner she got this over with, the sooner she would be able to return home. Hopefully she would have a satisfying report to give her Felix. She already respected the male and felt him to be fair. All she needed now was to obtain his agreement and a proposed date for him to take over.

Normally she didn't make snap decisions of this magnitude, but everything inside of her said this was a good male who would be fair and just but demand obedience. He was exactly what they needed.

"My Felix is advancing in age, Sire. He doesn't want just anyone taking over the Leap. He's anxious about this since there are several feline groups showing interest in his health and asking questions about other mature males in our family." Taylor paused to arrange her next statement a bit differently than she'd previously planned. "One of those groups is a Pride. It's well known that the Leo of a Pride will get rid of the older males when he takes over another group. Sometimes he just runs them out, and sometimes he kills them. This particular Leo seems to prefer the latter."

Taylor waited to let that sink in before she said any more. She wanted to watch his reactions so she could tell if he was even interested in what she was placing in front of him. It was a more than a generous offer since he'd essentially take over their Leap without bloodshed and step into a well-appointed home and a solid business, at least on their part.

"If this Leo is set on enlarging his territories, he won't accept anyone stepping in to take over without a fight," the Shadow's leader pointed out.

Taylor held back a sigh. He was sharp and picked up on that immediately. She'd hoped he wouldn't until after their initial discussion.

"True, but you'll have the complete backing of our felines, and it's rumored you are fearless and without equal. You've never lost a battle or suffered a serious injury as the result of one. We're confident you wouldn't have any trouble in this one either."

Despite not having to fight her Felix, he may well still have to fight to keep his position as their leader. It wasn't unheard of for a new Felix to need to fight two, sometimes three times before the other challengers gave up and walked away.

Taylor realized it had become more and more difficult to ignore the scandalizing pull of the jaguar just behind her chair. At some point he'd crept closer. It was all she could do not to turn around and slide herself up and down his hard, hot body. This was more than the usual sexual awareness and need that all feline breeds experienced now and then. Taylor was super aware of the male behind her. Plus, all of her nerve endings were hypersensitive so that the faint whiff of his breath as it reached the back of her neck ruffled the tiny hairs there. She could almost feel his sharp teeth as he held her still before mounting her.

"Miss Dristal. Taylor. Are you okay?"

Taylor jerked at the sound of her name from the Felix's mouth. His amused tone suggested that he knew very well what was wrong with her. The heat that burned in her cheeks only added to her embarrassment. Felines didn't get upset over something so natural. It was just a part of who they were, but she sure as hell was for some reason. Maybe it was because she normally didn't lose track of a conversation over a little sexual attraction.

"Yes. I'm fine."

"Please tell me more about your Leap and why your Felix wishes to court my shadow to take over his Leap."

"There are very few adult males in our leap now. This means there are far fewer births, which means we're going to die out if we don't find mates soon. Add to that, my Felix is old and dying and you can see that we are in desperate need of leadership that will keep us safe from rival groups who wish to take over."

"I can understand this need. So there are none strong enough within your Leap to take over?"

"No."

"Why wouldn't you want one of the other feline groups taking over your Leap?" the Felix asked.

"The only one interested is the lion's Pride. Their Leo is very dangerous. He'll kill any male in our Leap who shows any alpha tendencies. He's also known for killing the male children to keep his bloodline dominant. It isn't a life any of us wish to live."

"Perhaps we should extend your stay a few days so I can ask questions if I have any before I make a decision on this generous offer."

Taylor couldn't suppress the soft moan when something warm and wet pressed against the back of her neck. A breath of air followed that, eliciting a shiver all the way down her spine before settling between her legs at her core. The vibrations seemed to stimulate her clit without it even being touched.

"Um, I'm not sure that would be a good idea. Is there anything more you wish to know?" Taylor clenched her fists so tightly that her nails bit into the palms of her hands. She was sure she smelled blood where she broke the skin.

"I think it's a very good idea if I'm going to take this request seriously. I will contact your Felix and arrange this. It will also give me an opportunity to talk with him and not you alone." The shadow's leader stood, indicating the matter was decided and she was being dismissed. He nodded at someone behind her with a knowing smile.

*Oh God, what have I gotten into? This is insane.*

While she didn't normally care who the male was that interested her cat when she was in need, this was far different. These weren't felines of her Leap. She didn't know them in the least. Somehow that made it seem even more exciting, and that worried her more.

*Something about this is all wrong. I'm losing control, and that isn't normal. What is this? Why am I aching inside like this?*

"Come with me, kitten. I will show you where you are to stay."

The deep raspy voice sealed her fate as her cat leaned back into the male, purring with pleasure.

## Chapter Three

Marco gritted his teeth as searing hot fire shot straight to his balls. If he hadn't been concentrating as hard as he was, it might have taken him to his knees. Never had another feline affected him this way. Whatever it was about her, Marco planned to find out and fuck it out of his system. Rubio would have a field day with this female who'd captured his cat's interest so completely.

His twin loved exploring a female's body with his mouth, his hands, and his tongue. Sometimes Rubio would make them come without ever touching their pretty pussy. It was a talent of his twin that Marco always benefited from. He couldn't wait to introduce his little kitty to him.

"Where are you taking me?" Her breathless voice washed over him like a cool breeze with the promise of a wild spring storm on its heels.

"You'll be staying at our home while you are here. It will protect you from unwanted advances. You're a very beautiful and desirable unclaimed female, so many males will want to approach you. We won't allow that to happen."

"And what about you? Are you going to approach me?" She attempted to turn around, but Marco didn't allow it, holding her in place with his massive hand at the nape of her neck. If she managed to look up at him with those amazing green eyes, he was sure they would end up on the ground right where they stood. She was that entrancing.

"You can bet your hot ass I'm going to approach you. Both of us will just as soon as I get you back to my lair."

"Both of you? What do you mean?"

Marco heard the first lift in her voice indicating fear. He didn't want her afraid, just on edge and aware. Fear didn't turn him on like it did some of his kind. He'd always detested those who would rile up a female then slowly get rough with them until their adrenaline was a flavor in their mouths they couldn't get enough of. Sometimes that obsession turned deadly. With the loss of females in their shadow, when a male killed a female, he wasn't just punished as before. Now he was exiled and never allowed to return to the shadow.

"Easy, little kitty. I'm talking about my brother and me. You don't need to fear us. We would never hurt you." He prayed his voice had lost some of its earlier growling quality. He wanted to ease her fears so she would be more open to allowing his brother to share with him.

"I'm not having sex with you or your brother. I'm not a slave to my cat. She will be just fine until we return home." Her voice quivered, despite her attempt at bravado. He admired her intentions, but if he were right, they wouldn't last.

"You'll be safe with us to protect you. The jungle can be unpredictable. Just relax and allow us to take care of you, little kitten." Marco tried to temper his smile but knew by the way her eyes widened and her jaw stiffened that he hadn't lost the predatory set of his mouth. He knew from experience that his lips had pulled back to reveal his teeth.

*Damn! Why can't I control myself around her? This feels almost like a mating, but those are rare among the Jaguar. I will see how my twin is around her. Two Jaguars would not permanently share a mate. Just the mating would be unusual.*

"Don't mind my snarly attitude, Taylor. It is just my cat's reaction to your pheromones. Just like you, I'm not a slave to my Jaguar." Marco sure hoped not.

He led her through the thinned part of the jungle where he and his sibling had their lair. It wasn't one of old, a mere cave or hollowed-out tree. Instead, they had a nice hand-built house with a thatched roof covered by large leaves of indigenous foliage. They changed these out periodically to assure they didn't end up with leaks from the almost constant rain of the jungle.

"What a lovely home. It blends in with the area around it." Her melodic voice struck chords deep within him—dark hungry chords he desperately needed to quell.

"Thank you. It's comfortable for two bachelor Jaguars. Please come in and meet my brother, Rubio." Marco placed a hand at the small of her back, resisting the urge to throw her over his shoulder to carry her into his and Rubio's home like some Neanderthal. His twin was going to tease him unmercifully if he noticed Marco's behavior.

"Rubio!" he called out. "We have a guest."

Marco knew the moment his brother walked into the room they were in trouble. Rubio's eyes widened even as he opened his mouth just enough to breathe in Taylor's scent. It exposed his teeth enough that Taylor couldn't help but notice the additional saliva even as he swallowed.

"Introduce me, brother. Who is this delectable morsel you've captured?"

"Rubio, careful. You'll scare her. She isn't from our shadow, so she isn't familiar with your over-the-top flattery." Marco lifted his brows, hoping Rubio would notice and be cautious.

"Rubio, this is Miss Taylor Dristal from the United States, Washington State, I believe. Taylor, this is my brother, Rubio. Do not pay attention to his flattery. He enjoys shocking the females here."

"You're twins. I wasn't expecting that." Taylor's voice made it clear she was astonished in learning this.

"We are a rare bird," Rubio said. His smile grew wider, but to Marco's relief, there were less teeth involved.

"I don't believe we've had twins in our Leap in more than twenty years." She turned a bit and looked from Marco to his brother then back again. "Remarkable. You really are identical."

"In our youth we were terrible with the adults. They never knew who was who, and we often played tricks on them. Not so much now." Rubio chuckled. "Unless we really try, our personalities are different, so most of the Shadow can now tell us apart."

"I don't know your personalities very well, but I can tell you apart by the way you stand and the lilt in your voice. Marco's speech is more matter-of-fact while yours is flamboyant and a bit less believable."

Rubio slapped his hand over his heart. "I'm hurt that you would think I'm not sincere in my compliments. You truly are a beautiful female. All of that rich, sable brown hair with just a hint of ginger brings out the green in your eyes, making them flash with laughter and, I bet, flame with passion."

To Marco's surprise, Taylor burst out laughing. "See what I mean. Your brother's right. It is over the top."

"Brother, she's got you pegged already." Marco grinned then took Taylor's elbow. "Let's see about something to eat. You're bound to be starved after the plane trip. They feed you nothing on those little planes."

Marco turned back to grin at the surprised expression coupled with his brother's mouth wide open. Rubio had just been bested. He could hardly wait to see what other tricks their little kitten had up her sleeve.

"We've got zebra in the freezer if you're interested, or I can defrost some imported beefalo if you'd rather stick to non-exotic meats." Marco stood next to their industrial-sized refrigerator/freezer and waited for her to speak.

"Zebra? Really? I'd love to try some. Not a lot though. My stomach is still a little queasy from that wind-up airplane I flew in on. I swear I could hear the engines whining like they were about to give out." She turned when Rubio walked up behind her.

Marco took out a couple of zebra roasts but paused to watch the sizzle between his brother and Taylor. He swore he could almost see the sparks flying. Taylor's eyes had widened as she took in his brother's body with a slow slide up and down it. Rubio's mouth had opened again, and saliva gave his teeth an extra shiny appearance. Taylor didn't look the least bit worried by the aggressive stance Rubio had taken towering over her.

Just when he was sure his brother would lean down and kiss her, Taylor leaned up and sniffed along the other male's neck. When she rubbed her cheek against Rubio's skin, Marco swore his twin was going to attack, but somehow he managed to take a step back, chest heaving with the effort he made at restraint. Marco was impressed.

"I think we should continue this after we've fed you, *chiquito*," Rubio told her in a husky whisper.

Marco grinned. This would work out perfectly, and once they had her under their spell, she would eagerly agree to mate them. He had no doubt now that she was perfect for them. Headstrong but easily brought under control. At least she seemed to be. Only time would tell, and Marco couldn't wait to test her limits.

* * * *

A fine shiver tickled down her spine as Taylor allowed Marco to steer her toward a chair at the round mahogany table. Its lustrous dark color suited them, as well as their space. Whatever was happening to her, she wasn't sure she wanted to put a stop to it. Not only was she super attracted to Marco but now she also found herself swaying under Rubio's attentions. Both brothers had her pussy dripping and her skin super sensitive. She had no doubt they could smell her desire.

Even as the two men worked to put a meal before her, she studied them a little closer. True, they were identical twins, yet she could already see little tells that pointed out their individuality. Marco stood just a little straighter and tended to hold himself in a slightly more regal stance while Rubio was more relaxed, not slouchy but seemed to flow into any situation or against any surface.

Sleek and sensual described both of them. However, Marco ruled his while Rubio used his. She couldn't help but be attracted to their differences. Would they make love differently, as well? She could see Marco commanding her pleasure while Rubio would coax it out of her.

*Yes. I will definitely enjoy them at least once before I go. I would be a fool not to feast on this bounty. Most of the felines I know would have already had them once or twice by now.*

Taylor had a little more restraint and a lot more self-respect. They would have to earn her capitulation. Yet she had no doubt they would in spades. She couldn't wait for the dance to begin. She'd never enjoyed two at one time. Perhaps there would be some merit to the idea.

"Zebra rare, *nene*. Would you like wine or something else?" Marco delivered a plate with a generous slab of the zebra cooked perfectly for her taste.

"Bottled water? My cat loves fresh stream water, but my human side prefers the clean taste of bottled." She smiled in case that insulted them. She had no intention of doing that, but she'd learned that locals often became offended at the smallest of things.

"Of course we have it. Believe it or not, we seem to have the same taste," Rubio purred then set a bottle of spring water next to her plate.

"Aren't you going to eat with me?"

"We would love to share with you, *chiquito*. However, we had already eaten when you arrived." Rubio joined her at the table on her right while his brother sat on her left.

Taylor cut a piece of the zebra and tasted it for the first time. It even tasted exotic with a flavor that had her mouth watering with pleasure. It didn't taste like wild deer or even rabbit or squirrel but had a stronger wild flavor than they had.

"Amazing! I love it. I can just imagine the taste in my feline form." When she looked up at Marco, it was to see a hint of pride with the lifting of the corners of his mouth. Rubio had a more basic expression that spoke of wild, kinky sex.

"You must allow us to take you hunting while you're here. You will love the chase as much as anything." Marco reached over with one finger and wiped a bit of juice from the corner of her mouth then sucked his finger as he closed his eyes.

Dear God, they were going to eat her alive if she didn't watch out.

Rubio handed her a napkin even as his eyes seemed to dance with laughter. Then the jaguar licked along his teeth from top to bottom and winked at her.

Oh, boy.

Taylor was only able to finish half of the large piece of meat. Much more and she would have been too full to move. To her delight, the two men cut the remaining portion and ate it in front of her. It was then that she realized the seriousness of their intentions. They were treating her as a potential mate. Providing food for her and waiting until she'd eaten her fill before finishing her leftovers. She needed to straighten them out on that as soon as possible.

But not just yet. She needed a nap. The long trip and the delicious meal had taken its toll on her. Even as she patted her mouth with the napkin and stood up, her eyes felt heavy.

"Ah, our little *pajarito* is nearly asleep on her feet, brother. Let's settle her in our room and let her rest." Rubio threaded his fingers through her hair and pulled just a bit before sweeping her up in his arms.

"Whoa! Put me down. I can walk on my own," she complained.

"Nonsense, why walk when you have two handsome and very strong jaguars who can carry you around?" Rubio was really pouring it on.

"You're always jumping ahead of things, Rubio. It is a wonder you aren't slapped more often." Marco's teasing voice was mirrored in his dark eyes.

Taylor watched him over Rubio's shoulder and swore he was stalking her from the kitchen the short distance to the bedroom. It thrilled her despite the weariness that washed over her from the long day.

Marco swept around them and pulled back the sheets of the massive bed just before Rubio settled her onto the amazing mattress. It seemed to not only support her but embrace her all at the same time. She would have to ask where they got it and order one for herself. She would sleep much better on this once she returned home.

"Mmm, very comfy," she murmured around a wide yawn. "Sorry."

"Nonsense. You're exhausted. You can sleep with no worries of anyone bothering you. We will keep watch," Marco told her as he patted the sheets into place.

There was that mating ritual again. They were promising to protect her while she rested. She really was going to have to set them straight—later.

"Do you think your Felix will take my Felix's offer? The threat is very real for us."

"I believe it is a very good chance he will, *cariño*. Now rest," Marco told her with a voice as smooth as…

# Chapter Four

"She's perfect. Who would have ever thought twins would be destined for the same mate?" Rubio growled.

"I still can't believe it's a true mating. Those happen so rarely these days. We've got our work cut out for us though. A lot of how we proceed depends on our Felix's decision. If he doesn't agree to the Felix's proposal, we will need to woo her to remain here. I'm not sure what the protocols are in the States when it comes to a cross-feline mating." Marco shook his head as he paced up and down the hall leading from the kitchen to their bedroom.

"First let's see what Jag decides. Then we can ask Diaz to intervene with their Felix if necessary.

"We have an even bigger challenge with our mate, brother. She'll resist us if we stay here. She will not want to leave her Leap and all of her family and friends. I can understand that since she'd also be moving to a strange land." Marco stopped pacing, and his head shot up. "Company, brother."

Rubio nodded at Marco, who slipped back down the hall to stand guard outside their bedroom door. Once his brother was settled, Rubio turned to the door just before someone knocked. He took one sniff and knew it to be their Felix's second, Diaz. He opened the door and nodded at the Jaguar standing on the other side.

"How are you, Diaz? Please come in." Rubio took one step back and to the side to let the other jaguar inside.

"Rubio. Where is Marco?" Diaz asked, a deceptive smile lifting the corners of his mouth.

"He is here but down the hall watching over our…" Rubio couldn't stop the hesitation in his voice. "Guest." It wasn't easy for him to not claim her as their mate.

"Ah, yes, that is one of the reasons I'm here." Diaz walked over to the living area and relaxed into a club chair, seeming as at ease as any predator would be when they have the upper hand.

"Don't beat around the bush, Diaz. What do you want?" Rubio dropped his normally easy façade.

Diaz lifted one dark brow, giving him a devilish appearance. The feline always enjoyed toying with others, but now wasn't the best time to do that when Rubio had his potential mate under their roof. Especially when it obviously concerned her.

"Very well." The feline dropped all pretenses at portraying the nonchalant second with nothing more than a request. "Jag is well aware that this female is probably Marco's mate. There were far too many pheromones from him for it to just be a mutual attraction. Yes, she reacted to me a little, but it was only due to the intense pull of so much testosterone in the room."

"She isn't just Marco's mate, Diaz," Rubio informed him with a sneer. He hadn't meant to bleed so much aggression into the room.

"Easy, Rubio. Are you sure? It would be easy for the pheromones from the two of them to influence you, as well. Perhaps you're just picking up on the attraction and—"

"She is mine!" Rubio roared. Then softer, "There is no mistake in this. It is an entirely different scent between us than that of her and Marco."

"I see. That may complicate matters then." Diaz sat forward on the edge of the chair. "Jag is more than likely going to accept this Felix's proposal. He talked with the other leader a little while ago concerning the process."

"What has this got to do with Taylor? It will be good if we move there. Then there won't be any problems to overcome other than courting our mate. What is the issue, Diaz?" Rubio was growing frustrated with the conversation. His mouth thinned into a tight line that pressed his lips against his teeth. It hadn't helped that Diaz had questioned the mating.

"The Felix sent Taylor in hopes that our Felix would mate her and unite their Leap with our Shadow."

Rubio would have attacked him had Marco not rushed to restrain him. He wanted to tear the other man limb from limb then move on to Jag. He would not take their mate. If necessary, they would leave and find their own place without the Shadow. With three of them, it wouldn't cut so deep to be without others.

"Rubio." Marco's snarling voice in his ear warned him to stand down. He knew his twin was right.

"Marco, let me go," he finally said, willing his voice to sound a bit calmer.

"I hope Jag knows that would be a bad idea," Marco told the other man.

Rubio wasn't sure how his brother could remain so calm under the circumstances. Yes, he'd always been the less volatile of the two of them, but this was their mate in the balance. Not a fucking kill or some other female.

"Marco, Jag is well aware of the potential mating, though I don't think he would have anticipated it would be between the three of you. Still, he needs to discuss this with you." Diaz looked over at Rubio. "Though I suppose it is between the two of you now."

"We can't leave Taylor unprotected. Once she has awakened, we'll come talk with Jag and settle this." Marco's voice held a steel tone Rubio had heard only a few times in their lives.

"You realize this puts our Felix in a very precarious position." Diaz stood with a cautious expression as his lips thinned into a tight line.

"We realize that it presents some difficulty with how to tell the Felix why he is not able to accept Taylor as his mate. I'm sure their leader will accept that she has true mates. Something so rare should never be interfered with." Rubio felt his brother's hand on his shoulder and took it as approval he'd been able to speak in a civilized tone.

Diaz lifted a brow before nodding. "I'll let Jag know you will be over once Taylor is awake."

"Taylor is awake and not at all happy with someone else deciding who I will and won't mate." They all whirled to find Taylor standing behind them with her hands fisted on her hips. "My Felix knows how I feel, so there must be some mistake in what your leader thought he heard." The anger in her voice reflected the fury coloring her face a soft red, with flames of pure hell flashing in her eyes.

Rubio was in awe of her in that moment. Their mate did indeed have *pasión* and a backbone they would do well to remember. His balls ached as his cock hardened at such a display. He wanted to go to her and drink deep of her intense emotions right then. He felt his brother's body tighten next to him. Marco would thoroughly enjoy bringing her to her knees in need of them. He would never break her spirt, just tap into it so she could fully enjoy their lovemaking.

"As for you two, I will address your claims later. No one, and I mean no one, tells, orders, or maneuvers me into anything that I am not fine with. Tell your leader we will be there once I've had time to freshen up. You might warn him of just how pissed I am while you're at it." Taylor turned on one heel and marched back into their bedroom before slamming the door.

Rubio winced, as did both of the other males. Maybe Marco should rethink the commanding-her part of their wooing. Being on the wrong end of her ire wouldn't be a good place to be. Especially if they hoped to gain her favor as well as her pleasure.

\* \* \* \*

Of all the lamebrained, stupid ideas her Felix had come up with over the last few years, this had to be one of the biggest he'd thought to put into action. The fact that the Felix was her great-uncle didn't even bare mentioning since he barely recognized her as a relative now. He much more preferred to use her as an ambassador and glorified personal assistant instead. Uncle Roger felt better about ordering her around if he only considered her as another feline under his rule and not his great-niece.

"I'll make sure he understands this time that I'm not part of any negotiation once I return home."

He had no idea just how far he'd pushed her. She would resign everything he'd appointed her to and move to the other side of their territory where one of her friends lived with her mate and new baby boy.

*I can't believe it. He knows how intolerant I am when it comes to arranged matings. I nearly got killed the last time.*

Her father had wanted her safe and protected when he'd learned he had one of the few fatal diseases that affected their kind. Feline cardiomyopathy affected the heart muscle and caused a deterioration, much like advanced aging. No one had been able to find a cure or even a method to slow the process down. He'd only a few months left and thought he was making the right decision for her.

Unfortunately, the feline male he chose had a mean streak no one had witnessed before. Well, no one but his family, who turned a blind eye until she approached the Felix. She would never allow that to be her fate again.

She heard the outside door open then close signaling the likely approach of the two conniving males she still had to set straight.

A soft knock startled her despite her expecting it. She almost didn't answer.

"What? I'm about to take a shower and change clothes. I don't want to see or smell either of you in this bedroom."

"We understand, *grillo*. We just wanted to let you know we'll be waiting in the living room when you're ready. No one will disturb you," Marco said through the door. "Oh and your overnight cases are in the closet on the right."

Taylor didn't bother answering him. Instead she opened the closet and found her bags just inside. She didn't bother taking them out. Instead she rummaged around and found what she needed and walked to the bathroom to clean up. Every muscle in her body screamed with tension. She needed to relax so that she didn't cause an international incident when she met with their Felix again.

"What was Uncle Roger thinking? Unbelievable!"

But she knew he was desperate to do right by his Leap. There weren't enough strong males to stand up to the other groups, and none who could step in and fight the Leo when he challenged for leadership over their Leap

The hot shower went a long way in calming her righteous anger, but it still wasn't enough to erase the bad taste in her mouth from all of the intrigue and betrayal she was faced with. There were too many felines involved and enough shifter politics to make her want to throw up. Taylor had never wanted any part of the intricacies of it. She'd traded in a death sentence for being her great-uncle's glorified gopher. Well, it looked like she was finally getting her just rewards.

"Maybe death would have been the best choice after all." But Taylor didn't really believe that. She had too great a will to survive.

*I wish my dad were alive to help me with this. Of course if he'd never died, I probably wouldn't be in this mess to begin with.*

Taylor's mom had disappeared when she was only two years old. Most of the Leap thought she'd run off, not happy with being her father's mate, but she'd left everything she had just like she planned to come back. She and her dad felt that something had happened to her. He'd never stopped believing that until the day he died.

Taylor dressed in the only thing she had that might pass as a power suit. The black slacks needed pressing, but she doubted the twins owned an iron. The blood-red blouse with three-quarter sleeves had no frilly lace or ruffles, so it looked a little less like a party outfit but dressier than the other blouses in her bag. Taylor hadn't expected to stay more than one night, if that.

One last look in the mirror, and she was ready to face the almighty Felix and her supposed mates. Really. She was.

# Chapter Five

"¡*Carajo*! This is bullshit." Rubio paced the length of the living room, only to stop next to the kitchen island and kick it.

"Cracking your foot and damaging the wood will do nothing to help in this situation, brother. Rein it in before our mate catches you acting a fool." Marco had never seen his twin this passionate about anything, much less a female. Yes, he often exaggerated and appeared much more emotional than Marco ever allowed himself to show, but this was more. Much more.

Of course this female wasn't just any female. She was their destined mate. Marco felt much the same way Rubio did but wasn't allowing his anger to overtake him. They had to appear confident and completely sure of themselves before they met with their Felix. Jag was fair, and though he didn't like politics and tended to leave that area up to Diaz when possible, he knew how to play the game. Marco just hoped he didn't plan to use their Taylor as a pawn like her Felix was doing.

"You're right, Marco. I know this, but my anger has my jaguar enraged. I wish we had time for a run. He isn't happy about not being let out to fight for his mate." Rubio shivered all over, his fingers releasing their razor-sharp claws before he managed to absorb them back inside.

"Rubio. *Mierda*! Calm down. If you lose control and shift, we will lose her for sure. No female will respect us if we have no control."

"*Está jodido*, Marco. I won't stand still and let Jag or Diaz take our mate. I will remain in control so Taylor won't reject us, but if our

Felix doesn't make it clear to her Felix that she is ours, we will take her and go." Rubio pulled himself up straight.

Marco was pleased and a little impressed as his twin regained complete control. Even his hair relaxed, and the muscles of his face lost their tenseness, his mouth no longer pulled back in a sneer. He'd wondered if the sneer was going to become a constant expression with as much as he'd seen it this day.

*Now that he is under control, I've got to get myself smoothed out. Times like this I wish alcohol worked on shifters. I don't need enough to dull my senses like so many humans tend to do, just enough to help me relax. Rubio will never let me live it down if I am the one to lose control.*

"Rubio, we will not lose our female. I honestly believe that Jag will make this right." Marco prayed he was right.

"And if the Felix insists on the mating before he will continue with negotiations? What then, brother? You and I both know that the good of the many will outweigh the three of us."

"And if after all of this Taylor refuses to accept us? What has it all been for?" Marco asked.

His twin's face tightened once again. Rubio's eyes narrowed, and when he spoke, his words were guttural. "She won't refuse us. You've felt her sway toward us. It would only be verbal defiance and would change given time."

Marco had a pretty good idea that his brother was correct, but how they treated their little *fénix* now would influence their future relationship with her. They couldn't risk making a mistake that costly before they'd even secured her acceptance.

"Marco, there is one other way to stop this from happening if our Felix doesn't agree." Rubio's face remained calm, though there was a narrowing of his eyes now.

"I'm not sure I want to ask what you're thinking."

Rubio's smile was all teeth. "If she is carrying our kit, she can't be forced to mate with anyone else. She may choose to, but she can't be used as a bargaining chip or forced by her Felix."

Marco couldn't stop the wide smile that poured over his face even as excitement raced through his veins. His cock was pretty damn happy with the idea, as well.

"I'm a little afraid of what you two are up to." Taylor's sensuous, sexy voice jerked them both around in an about-face. "Yep. Up to something, and I bet I'm not going to like it. Am I?"

Marco had to rethink how to breathe then how to form words. That outfit would make a dead feline sit up and beg, and cats didn't beg. The black slacks hugged every amazing curve on her body. That ass! He wanted to see it walking away from him just once. Then she had to always walk toward him. The dark slacks accented her soft, rounded belly that would swell with their kits one day if he had any say in the matter. Even now he wanted to rub his face all over her body.

"*Nene*, you are stunning. I am at a loss for words." Rubio's eyes followed her every move.

Marco understood why. Each move she made had the silky material of her blouse flashing a bit of skin here or a curve of her breast there. It seemed to move with her as if it were alive. No doubt it was so happy to be next to her skin that it caressed her with each movement of her body.

*I would die a happy cat if I could be that blouse for one night.*

"Let me see you, Taylor. You are a vision in red." Rubio smiled and held out his hand. "That color brings out the green in your eyes so that they shine like the richest of emeralds. Yes, emeralds are the jewels you should be draped in."

"There you are with the flattery again, Rubio. How can someone ever believe you if you spread it so thick all the time?" she asked with a quiet laugh.

"He's right, *grillo*. Emeralds were created with you in mind. The fire in them would look amazing sprinkled among the fiery curls that frame your amazing face. It would be a sin to deny them their greatest wish." Marco was as surprised as his twin was at the grandiose flattery that had slipped from his lips. He didn't do niceties. He was much more to the point when it came to females.

*She's not just any female. She's our female. Mate!*

"*Mueve tus caderas*, sweetness. Walk toward Marco. I want to see your luscious ass sway in those amazing pants. Your body was made to be worshiped." Rubio didn't seem to have an off switch when it came to Taylor. Marco now understood why.

"Will you allow us to hold you for just a minute, *chiquito*?" Marco cringed inside. Even to him it sounded as if he were begging.

"Hold me?" Taylor actually looked confused.

"Yes. We want to touch you and assure that no one will bother you," Marco explained.

"Ah, you wish to scent mark me like some piece of property you own. You don't own me, *el gato*!"

"It's *el felino*, Taylor." Marco took a step closer to her.

"What? *Gato* is cat. I remember my high school Spanish classes very well." She took a step back.

Marco smiled as Rubio move behind her. She would back into him if she took another step. Perfect.

"*Gato* is for a house cat, not a wild cat. I think that you would agree that neither Rubio or myself are domesticated. We are called, *el felino*, wild and free.*" He took that next step in her direction, knowing she would take a step back and into his brother's arms.

"Wild? Yes, that fits the two of you to a tee." Her voice sounded husky and inviting, and she took that step back.

Rubio brought his arms around her and nuzzled his face into her neck. "You smell good enough to eat *pequeño ratón*."

Her eyes grew wide and slightly dilated as his brother mouthed her neck and the back of her ear. Marco watched as her eyes closed even as she let her head drop back onto his brother's shoulder.

*Gracias a Dios,* but she was hot as hell. He could smell her arousal and knew that if he checked, she'd be slick with her desire. *Dios,* he wanted to check.

"What are you doing to me?" she choked out.

She didn't pull away or open her eyes.

Rubio kept his eyes on Marco as he ran both hands down either side of her body, pausing only a second at her breasts before dipping to her hips, where he squeezed them before moving back up just as slowly. This time, when he reached her breasts, Rubio slid his hands around to cup them just as he flicked his tongue at her earlobe.

"Holly hell!" Taylor arched into Rubio even as her eyes flashed open.

"Easy, *cariño*," Rubio crooned. "It's all good."

Marco stepped closer, eager to get his taste before her arousal faded, and she pulled back. He didn't use his hands, allowing Rubio to gentle her. Instead, he leaned in and rubbed his cheek along hers then around her chin to the other side.

Her scent sent him into a cold sweat in an effort not to drag her away from Rubio and slam her against the wall so he could take her and make her theirs. Just the idea of sliding his dick into her slippery, sweet pussy nearly had him coming in his jeans. There was no doubt he'd have a wet spot on the front of them by the time he managed to back away.

"She smells like the sweetest of flowers, Marco. I'm intoxicated just holding her. I don't want anyone to get anywhere near her." Rubio growled out the last sentence in a warning for both Taylor and him.

Marco leaned in again and licked along her lower lip, wanting to suck it into his mouth to tease and torment but knew that would lead to other things, things they couldn't start right then.

Later.

"It's time, brother. Give her space so she can regain control. We don't want her this overcome with other males around. We'll have to kill some of our friends if they can't control themselves." Marco leaned away from her and took several steps back to clear his head of the tempting morsel standing right in front of him.

Rubio nodded and stepped away, as well. He kept one hand at her waist to keep her steady until all of the pheromones in the air dissipated and she could think again. Marco dreaded that moment when she realized what had been happening between the three of them. It was natural and normal for all felines, but he wasn't sure how their mate would deal with it, with them for that matter.

* * * *

Taylor's head cleared enough that she could think without the cloying scents of male musk affecting her mind. She really had to talk to them about their teaming up on her like that. She had no doubt now that they were true mates. It was something Taylor hadn't heard of occurring in her Leap in over twenty-five years. Maybe longer than that.

Until she'd experienced the overwhelming need that had her squeezing her thighs together, she hadn't believed their claim. The entire time she'd been in the shower Taylor had denied it was true. Even while she dried off and dressed, she'd thought about how to explain to them that she wasn't their mate and wouldn't be staying in Central America. All of those plans and ideas swirled away in the ebb and flow of the tide that had her securely tied to two arrogant male jaguars. Well, she wasn't theirs. They were hers.

She snapped her eyes open and shook Rubio's hand from her waist. Both males watched her as if she were a rabid crocodile with a friendly smile. Not a bad analogy actually. Taylor smoothed down her blouse then slid her hands down the sides of her slacks before propping her hands on her hips and narrowing her eyes at them.

"Next time we are going to an important meeting like this, don't touch me beforehand. It wrinkles my outfit and gives the other males the idea that they go through you to get to me. Maybe in some things, but not business. Do you understand?"

She bit her lips to keep from smiling as both jaguars seemed to shake themselves in an effort to figure out what had just happened. She would need to keep them off their paws if she were to make a go of their mating. Once they managed to hold complete confidence concerning her, she'd lose a measure of control over them. She would need to be in control for this to work. There were, after all, two of them.

She cleared her throat and lifted a brow as she waited for them to settle into some form of normality.

"We like having you wear our scent," Rubio growled. He took a step in her direction.

Taylor held up one hand. "Your scent will be all over me at some point, and this need to freshen it won't be necessary. Anything other than business and I won't fuss—too much—but business is non-negotiable. *¿Entendido?*"

Marco chuckled. "Loud and clear."

"Rubio?" Taylor watched the other male. He was the more volatile of the two jaguars and less predictable than Marco.

"You actually remembered something from your Spanish classes. I'm impressed." Rubio, the asshole, bowed.

"We have a lot to talk about after this meeting, *cariño.*" Marco's statement sounded more like a promise than anything else.

*Yes, we do have a lot to discuss. I don't know how the female jaguars are treated here, but I will be treated with more than sexual respect. I'm a businesswoman who is just as business savvy as any male.*

Taylor watched Marco casually lean against the kitchen island as if he hadn't been as fired up as she'd been only a few seconds ago. A small part of her worried that these two had the same instincts as their cousin jaguars in the wild despite the evidence supporting that it was a true mating. Would they actually settle down to be a family? What about when there were cubs to feed?

Few jaguar males took permanent mates. Even in the US they were well known to play the love-them-and-leave-them game. Few females would deal with them because of it, but still, there were always those who thought they could tame the wildness within them, and they were usually wrong.

*Why do I think I will have any better chance at taming one, much less two?*

"Whoa, Taylor. What are you thinking about right now? You're frowning." Marco walked over to where she hadn't moved since they'd stopped playing with her. "We don't like frowning."

She shook her head and tried to step around him. Rubio stood in her way this time.

"Talk to us, Taylor. There should never be secrets between us. Our relationship will only work if we're all completely honest with our feelings."

Rubio's voice seemed as steady as Marco's had. They were in complete control it seemed. It strengthened her case that they wouldn't be as emotionally committed to their mating as she inevitably would be. Especially when she became pregnant. With miscarriages among her Leap so high, she could only pray that she would be able to carry them to term.

*Stop it! I haven't mated them yet, much less become pregnant. Already they have me wanting what I might never be able to have.*

"Taylor?" Marco's voice held a promise of something if she didn't comply.

Oddly enough, she didn't fear him. Not like before. He didn't come across as angry with her as he'd been with his Felix earlier. That in itself relaxed her worries just a bit.

"How do I know that you will honor the mating if we go through with it?" she finally asked.

"You doubt us?" Rubio's face tightened so that his eyes narrowed enough that Taylor did get a bit worried.

"Sorry, jaguars have a very trashy reputation in the US. How many of your friends are settled into long-term relationships? How many have actually taken a mate?" she asked.

Rubio sighed as his face deflated. He and his brother exchanged guilty looks. She'd been right. They weren't going to be able to settle down with just her. Pain started a grumble in her gut even as a sour taste filled her mouth.

"You're right. Most male jaguars don't spend any time with a female even when they have their cubs. They are not us. We've always hoped to find someone to settle down with and have a family. We love keeping cubs around to play with but want our own." Marco reached out and took her hand.

Taylor let him.

"The mating only seals this for us. We aren't the wandering kind. We have a permanent home and had no intentions of ever moving. If our leaders can agree on terms, we will move to America with you. If not, we would want you to remain with us, here, where we have business interests so we can take care of you."

It stung when Rubio didn't reach out to take her other hand. He seemed to need coaxing after her assumptions that they would play with her then leave once they'd had their fill. No one could blame her considering the jaguars' history. Still, the male needed assurance that she didn't lump him in with the rest.

"I believe you, Marco. Rubio, I'm sorry if I insulted you, but I had good reason to doubt your sincerity, true mating or not."

Rubio nodded, but the uncertainty hadn't left his eyes. Truly, Taylor hadn't believed the male could be hurt. She should have known that beneath all of the bravado and compliments lay the heart of an insecure male. It made her see him and all of his flattery in a different light.

She had no time to coax the laughter back into his eyes with the threat looming over their heads. They needed to see the Felix and set him straight.

# Chapter Six

Rubio followed his brother with their mate situated between them as they approached the Felix's home. He prepared himself for a fight. His brother might think Jag would let them mate Taylor, but Rubio didn't like the odds. The needs of the many over the needs of a few. Jag had to think about all of his shadow.

The door opened before Marco had lifted his hand to knock. "Sire is waiting for you." Diaz appeared a little uneasy, which didn't bode well for them. Rubio prepared himself for bad news and the need to fight to protect his mate.

"I don't like this," Rubio muttered under his breath. He knew the other jaguars could hear him, but he didn't much care.

They walked through the double doors that had been left open today. When they entered the office, Diaz closed them then took his place just to the right and behind their Felix. An uneasy silence settled over them until finally their Felix sighed and shook his head.

"I know Diaz has told you about the mating proposal by the Felix of the leopards." Jag stood up in one fluid movement then walked around the large ornate desk to pull open a hidden drawer on the end of the desk. Inside appeared to be several envelopes and books. He selected one of the books then closed the drawer.

Instead of sitting back down behind his desk, Jag leaned against the front of it and opened the book. He paged through it for a few seconds then located whatever he'd been looking for. When he looked up, the seriousness in his eyes had Rubio fidgeting, itching to say something, but he managed to keep his tongue.

Marco's agitation bled all over him though. For once his always-in-control brother stood in the same boat that he did. The threat to their mating had both jaguars protesting the tight control he and his brother had on them. God help anyone who got in their way if they managed to break through.

"As Diaz has informed you, the Felix of the Washington Leap would like to offer it to me, giving us a place to live without the constant pressures of the cartel of the month bearing down on us. In exchange, we would provide protection to those we inherit in the process and there is no bloodshed to accomplish this." Jag sighed but continued. "At issue is his request that I mate with his great-niece, Taylor, to seal our groups together as a show of good faith. In other words, he believes that if I am married into the family, I'll be less likely to do away with any of them."

"I trust that you informed him that was not possible," his brother bit out.

"Not exactly."

"Why the hell not?" Rubio spoke up this time. "She's our mate. A true mating. You can't possibly plan to deny us that!"

"What I plan is what I plan and not up for negotiations." The Felix didn't yell, but the bite in his words spoke for him.

The hairs along Rubio's skin stood up as their Felix bled power throughout the room. The rage flashing in his eyes, the only other outward sign of his anger with them. Rubio fought his jaguar to restrain himself before he made things worse. When he risked a glance in his brother's direction, it was to find censure there, as well.

While they'd been arguing, their mate had been strangely quiet. They looked back to where they'd left her standing when they'd walked in to find her gone.

"Taylor!" Rubio turned to open the door to look for her, finding that she'd stepped just outside to use her cell phone.

She paced back and forth as she held the cell phone to her ear. Nothing hid the frown that pulled at the corners of her mouth or the flashing in her eyes that betrayed just how angry she was. The more she listened, the faster her steps.

"I know we had an agreement, but it didn't include you auctioning me off to the highest bidder! I won't do it. You can't make me either. I'll walk away from the Leap in a heartbeat before I allow you to manipulate me this way."

Rubio and his brother exchanged glances. Their mate was taking things into her own hands. Jag coughed to grab their attention once again. They were hard-pressed to take their eyes off her.

"I found a reference in the journals of our ancestors that spoke of this," he began. "If a mate is found that has been promised to another, exceptions can be granted provided the female doesn't produce a kit after one year."

"You're telling us that you would keep her for a year then release her to us after that year is up? No way in hell! She's our true mate, Jag. We'll fight for her, leave for her. Why is it necessary for you to take her when you're willing to take on their Leap without it?" Marco had been silent until this.

"Marco's right. That's bullshit. If they need someone to stand for them, they don't have the luxury to make demands." Rubio couldn't believe that Jag was actually taking the Felix's demands seriously. He was the one with the power in this situation.

"Forget it! I'm not doing it. Either rescind the offer or I won't be returning home. I'll stay with my mates here, and you can get by however you can. You think about that and get back to me."

Their Felix winced when she started to throw her phone against the wall but chose to keep it and throw her purse. Still, something inside the purse smashed by the sound it produced when it hit the wall.

"I take it that didn't go well," Marco murmured.

"What made you come to that conclusion?" The sarcasm in her voice aroused his cat, who wanted nothing more than to pounce on her.

"Perhaps you should repeat that, Sire. I don't think Tayler heard what you said." Diaz's smirk set his mate's anger up a notch higher if that were possible.

Their Felix didn't seem to care that she was already steaming after her conversation with her great-uncle. He repeated what he'd just told them. Oddly enough she calmed down and seemed to think about it. That upset Rubio's cat even more. No way would he allow her to mate with Jag. A year was too long to wait regardless. Just thinking about her in Jag's arms shot red to his eyes and the discolored haze changed the way he viewed everything and everyone in his path.

"Rubio. Control, brother. Calm the hell down. *Dios*!" Marco's hold was shaky at best.

Rubio listened to his brother but wasn't sure how long he could continue to do so. "Fucking shifter politics! When we settled here, you assured us we wouldn't have to deal with it anymore."

"If you'd all shut your mouths and listen, I think I have an answer to the situation. Just calm the hell down. Now!" Jag's deep voice vibrated off the walls.

He and Marcus stilled, reacting to their Felix's power. Oddly enough, Taylor wasn't as affected, though she did close her mouth.

"Instead, we turn it the other way around. She is with you for one year, and if she isn't able to produce a kit, then she would revert back to me." He rubbed at the back of his head. "Right now they're holding their breath for the next surge of Felix wannabes. Time is ticking for them."

"I don't believe this. Either I've got to get pregnant with my mates, or I have to not get pregnant with you so I can be with my mates. I don't exactly see the point in all of this."

Neither did Rubio, but then he wanted her and by any means necessary. However, that didn't include their Felix mating her and taking her away from them.

"What happens when I don't get pregnant?" They could barely hear Taylor this time.

Their Felix hesitated before answering her. "Then you would return to me under the contract."

"No!" Both Rubio and his brother erupted at the same time. "That is not going to happen."

"You can't guarantee that I will get pregnant within a year. I'm not taking that chance. I refuse to be a pawn in his game. If he truly wants to protect his Leap, he will go through with the transfer without adding me to sweeten the pot. I won't be used as a pawn." Taylor grabbed her purse from off the floor and stomped out the office leaving them to talk it out without her.

"You're not seriously considering this, are you?" Marcus still didn't seem to believe any of it could be real.

"Look, this isn't what I want to deal with either, but the offer to run their Leap so that we can continue to lead a normal life without another group telling us what we can and can't do is ideal for our needs. No one wants to stay here any longer. There's been too much death and too many hunters here to kill the beasts who have, one by one, taken out the cartel members." Jag pulled at his hair then sat back down.

"The Felix has looked for a way out for you. I would think you'd be grateful that he's even tried." Diaz reprimanded them for their audacity in chastising him.

"Don't patronize us. You took great pleasure in announcing that back at our home. You knew how it would affect us, and you did it without one ounce of empathy. One day you'll screw with the wrong cat, Diaz." Marcus took a threatening step toward the other shifter. "But then again, maybe you already have." Rubio managed to hold him back, but it took a scuffle before he had the other male's attention.

"Stop it, all of you. This isn't the time for petty displays of aggression. We have a dilemma that must be addressed and soon. The Felix's days are numbered, and though he assures me he doesn't care if he lives or dies at this point, he just wants his cats settled and safe.

Apparently he still has some relatives he's fond of." Jag pulled the old book across the desk to leaf through it some more.

"We can guess which of them he isn't as fond of," Marco muttered.

"You hold the power, Sire. Why are you playing his game? He hasn't got another option, or he wouldn't have sought us out all the way to Central America. There's nothing stopping you from taking his Leap by force anyway." Rubio prowled back and forth as he watched his Felix.

"Actually there is." Jag sighed and closed the book. "We can't cross into the US without a sponsoring shifter group. If we don't agree to his demands or find another way to settle this, he will deny our petition for entry."

Rubio stopped pacing and stared at the other male. "Seriously? We aren't allowed to freely travel to the US?"

"Remember, they acknowledge us as sentient beings with free will and the ability to control our animal sides. We will have rights in the US, but it comes at a price. We have to have another shifter group vouch that our intentions for traveling there are good and without plans to cause trouble. Without that, we would have to go the long road of petitioning the government for asylum. That will take more time than I believe we have." Jag steepled his fingers as he talked.

"I'm beginning to wonder if we'd be better off remaining here and taking over the cartels instead of just living here and taking what they dish out." Rubio's growl gave his words a biting quality. "We need to find Taylor and make sure she doesn't try to return home to slice and dice her great-uncle."

"What I'd like to know is what she meant when she told him over the phone that an arranged mating hadn't been in the agreement," Marco said. "The agreement to come here and talk to you, Jag, or is there something else going on we're not aware of?"

"I'll leave that to you two to discover when you catch her again." Their Felix gave them a tired smile before continuing to read. "I'll keep looking for another way out of this mess. In the meantime, it would behoove you two to bed her and often."

Diaz shook his head. "She didn't look convinced about that possibility either, Sir. Maybe she believes that she is sterile as so many of our females are now."

"Let's hope not for all of our sakes." Jag lifted an eyebrow in Diaz's direction. "You, too, my friend. She won't discriminate if something doesn't give. I'm not so sure you have it in you to survive a tongue-lashing like she'll no doubt give all of us."

\* \* \* \*

*I'll rip his heart out and punch holes in his lungs for this. He had no right to use me as a pawn when he knew my past.*

Then her great-uncle had never much cared for her in the first place. The only kind thing he'd ever done for her was dissolve the mating between her and her abusive mate. She'd had to subject herself to his beatings on five different occasions and have a witness come forward to prove her claims. Since shifters were often violent during sex, the bruising would be commonplace and easily explained away.

Now she had to be sure and get pregnant by her mates so that she could remain with them as their mate. How many ways could it get any more fucked up? The worse part of it all was that they were her true mates, and she wasn't sure she could get pregnant. Two years with her ex hadn't produced a kit, and with the decline in pregnancies among their Leap, she was afraid that she would be one of those who'd ended up sterile.

The thought of allowing the arranged mating to continue, the disappointment of not being able to become pregnant, then the mandate that she leave her true mates and take their Felix as a mate was enough stress to prevent even a fertile leopard from carrying a kit. What was she going to do?

*Run.*

That one word sounded so simple but held major consequences should she decide to do it. Living out in the human world without a Leap to fall back on, or take comfort from, would not only put her at risk among the humans but also make her fair game to other unmated male shifters searching for a female.

*I can't ask my true mates to leave everything they know to go with me. They would offer, but I'll just refuse.*

Honestly, did she think she had a choice where those two were concerned? She talked a big game, but the truth of the matter was that they held sway over her heart, so everything else in her world would fall into step behind them.

There just had to be another way to settle the problem without bloodshed or losing their place in their shadow. The thought of them saying good-bye to all of their friends and any family they might have among their people broke her heart. They'd talked of caring for some of the kits in their home and how much they wanted kits of their own someday. Tayler couldn't see relegating them to a life without something they dearly wanted. Nor could she see leaving them if she didn't get pregnant to go to their Felix. That would be equally cruel for them.

*I'm damned if I do and damned if I don't agree to this crazy scheme.*

One thing she'd learned growing up in the political unrest of a shifter group was that she could never depend on anything turning out the way she'd planned it. That proved even truer when someone thought they could circumvent the issue by using trickery.

*How many times have I tried to escape some task my uncle assigned me and the punishment was far worse than if I'd completed it in the first place?*

Taylor still didn't believe that her mom had just walked out one day to never look back. She'd loved her mate and her daughter. There was a story behind her disappearance, and she was sure her great-uncle knew what it was. He and her father had never gotten on despite her father refusing the position as Felix. Instead, her father watched and waited for his mate until the day he died. He was a huge, proud leopard who refused to believe the worst about others. Her father was the one others went to for money or for a sandwich if they were without.

Suddenly she wanted to run, not necessarily away but run to let her leopard free for a while. As if on cue, her leopard growled to be let out, but Taylor didn't know the jungle and all of its hidden dangers. She'd just have to wait until the others finished planning her future for her.

The short walk back to the twins' home helped clear her head enough that she could think without a red haze filling her sight. This time she couldn't figure any way out of the mess she'd landed in. The idea of being forced into a mating turned her stomach. It wasn't just her who would suffer this time. The twins would go insane if she was forced to accept their Felix as her mate.

Taylor held no illusions that they were madly in love with her, but a true mating involved more than just lust and need. Mates began imprinting on each other the moment they met. Their hearts beat as one, and separation was like a part of you died while the other part had to continue going through the motions of living. She knew. She'd watched her father slip away into a shell of his former self.

There had to be some way to stop her great-uncle's ludicrous plan. If what the old cat had told her was true, the Leap had very little time left before one of the other groups struck.

"Taylor!" Marco's voice held panic.

Before she could answer him, Rubio called out, as well.

"Taylor! Where are you?"

She walked to the door and threw it open. "I'm here. I haven't gone out into the jungle to run, but I was tempted. I'm not stupid though. I know there are more dangers out there than I could possibly imagine."

Two enormous males attacked her, trapping her between them as they growled and rubbed their cheeks all over her. She didn't try to stop them. They needed this, and if the truth were told, so did she. Already her cat yearned for their touch, and the first touch of their bodies to hers set off a chain reaction that started out as dizzying relief but quickly morphed into a fierce, burning need.

"What is your Felix going to do?" she managed to ask when she could breathe again.

"He's not sure. Jag is a fair leader. He knows the value of a true mating and that if it should happen that you don't become pregnant, taking you from us would cause a war and tear our families apart." Marco stepped back just enough for Rubio to touch more of her.

"What are the options? If we left, would he still take over the Leap from my Felix? I don't want you to have to give up your friends and family though." Taylor dug her hands in Rubio's thick hair.

"Ease back, brother. Let's talk. We need to get this out of the way." Marco tugged on her hand until Rubio released his hold and followed them over to the couch.

"There aren't a lot of options." Rubio sat on one side of her and turned so he could see her face. "Your Felix wants some measure of assurance that our Felix won't tear apart his Leap once the exchange has been completed. He'd have no recourse should Jag decide to follow the history of conquered groups and kill off the young males to prevent them from challenging him. He could do anything he wanted to, and short of issuing challenge and fighting to keep his Leap, your uncle wouldn't be able to stop him. We all know he couldn't win that fight."

Marco held on to one of her hands, and his tantalizing scent teased her nose, causing her cat to purr. It evidently pleased Marco since he purred right along with her. For an instant, Taylor felt how it could be, how it should be for them. Then reality crashed over her in the form of an image of Jag above her. Her stomach rolled.

"The only other option our Felix could think of was to challenge your Felix and take the Leap by force. Then you'd be under no obligation to follow through with any treaty. It isn't an ideal choice since some of your Leap will fill honor bound to step in and fight. Though I'm sure your leopards are strong and good fighters, our jaguars are lethal and better than any other shifter group in a fight." Marco's claim wasn't unwarranted.

The jaguar had always been at the top of the shifter food chain. In addition, they lived in a dangerous jungle where they were constantly fighting for their lives. The leopards rarely fought for anything other than pleasure or to settle a dispute.

"I don't want to be the cause of others getting hurt or killed." Taylor hated the position her Felix had put her in. "Some of the leopards who would fight alongside of him are my friends and my friends' mates."

"It is not your call, *nene*. Therefore, you have no reason to feel responsible regardless of his decision." Rubio rubbed the back of his knuckles along her jaw. "I don't like seeing you upset."

"What are we going to do while he makes his decision?" She didn't like just sitting around but could tell the males didn't want her out running yet. Perhaps they were right since, in her agitation, she could easily get into trouble before she realized it.

"Ah, sweet Taylor. *Te necesito*." Rubio stood up, drawing her up and into his arms. "Until there is a course of action, we shall create our own action and plot our own course."

Taylor's brows lifted in understanding. They had no intentions of waiting around while their Felix contemplated options. The answer to their problem had already been identified as far as her males were concerned. All that was left was to strip and fuck until they either died of dehydration and exhaustion or they scented the change in her if she conceived.

*Please let me conceive.*

# Chapter Seven

Taylor wanted the twins. She'd fought the mating call, but there was no reason to continue that now. Her Felix had backed her into a corner, and cats didn't like corners. If she'd any chance of staying with her true mates, she had to get pregnant and fast. She didn't want the Jaguar Felix to challenge her great-uncle and risk losing friends because of it.

"If you like what you have on, *mi amor*, take it off. Now!" Rubio watched her as she backed down the hall to the bedroom.

"If he doesn't tear it off of you, I will, *nene*." Marco stalked toward her until her back hit the bedroom door.

"I'm taking it off." She unbuttoned the blouse. "See?"

Her heart skipped a beat at the sight of both males licking their lips as they watched her remove the blouse in slow, sensuous movements meant to entice. She wasn't disappointed. Before she could get the door opened very wide, they pounced.

"The blouse is safe, Taylor, but the rest will suffer." Rubio held out one hand, and razor-sharp claws extended from his fingertips.

"Just the clothes, brother. Don't scratch that beautiful skin. I want to paint her with my tongue." Marco walked around her as Rubio moved closer.

Taylor gasped with surprise when Marco caught her wrists in his hands and pulled them behind her so that her chest poked forward, her breasts heaving against the lacy red bra. His breath heated her neck as he whispered words and phrases she didn't understand in her ear.

Rubio ran one claw down her shoulder next to the bra strap then flicked his wrist so fast she wasn't even aware of it until that strap dropped from her shoulder. He followed up by cutting the other strap before she'd recovered from the first. He tilted his head so that the light caught the change in his eyes. They were a bright gold that flashed when he bared his sharp teeth in a feral smile.

"You are so hot, *cariño*. I can feel your heat beating against my skin." Rubio growled. "Hold still while I help you out of your pants."

Taylor knew better than to even breathe as the male jaguar ran the razor-sharp claw from her waistband down to her ankle. He reversed on the other leg, and they fell to land in a heap around her feet.

Marco nipped her shoulder. "My turn, brother."

Rubio snarled but turned her to face Marco when he let go of her wrists. Now Rubio gripped them with both hands as he licked a path from just behind her ear down her neck, where he nipped her shoulder as his brother had.

"Ah!" Taylor tried not to make a sound, but when Marco pushed a curved claw into her cleavage then snatched it through the material of her bra, she was helpless.

His satisfied smile promised more of that to come and no sooner had she thought than he teased the outside of her thighs with his claws, slowly pulling them upward then jerking them through either side of her thong so that it, too, drifted to the floor. They had her where they wanted her, naked and aroused to the point of panting.

Her turn.

Taylor smiled up at Marco before spinning around to tear Rubio's shirt from his body, ripping it down the center so that buttons flew, bouncing across the floor. She'd always wanted to do that. It was much more fun than she'd imagined.

Before Rubio could get over his surprise, she twisted to one side and caught Marco by surprise, shredding his shirt from behind.

*Oops. I think I nicked him a little. Yummy. Blood—flesh.*

She ran her tongue up the small scratch then bit the back of his shoulder just enough to leave red marks but not break the skin.

"She's a little *gato salvaje*. We will need to watch out for her, brother." Rubio chuckled. "Hold her still while I finish undressing."

Taylor started to pull away, but Marco wrapped his arms around her, pulling her tight against him. Her chest heaved in excitement as well as a healthy dose of trepidation. A male caught up in the feral heat of a female could injure her. She didn't think the twins would lose control, but then she didn't really know them yet.

"Easy, *gato*. We will take care of you. Watch Rubio undress. See how hard he is for you."

Rubio watched her as he lowered his jeans past his hips. Taylor inhaled through her mouth to catch the first scent of his arousal. When his cock sprang free, every drop of saliva dried up at the length and width of him. He stepped out of his jeans, looked down, and stroked his dick from root to tip. A bead of cum pearled at the slit, and just like, that her mouth was no longer dry. When he looked up, his eyes had grown darker. The wicked cat ran his tongue over his teeth as he squeezed his cock at the base then pulled on it all the way to the tip once again.

"Oh God." Taylor couldn't quite catch her breath.

"I've anticipated this moment since my first glance of you. When your scent hit me, I nearly lost control and pounced." Marco sucked on her earlobe as he ground his pelvis against her ass.

Since they were identical twins, and from the feel of him against her body, Taylor was sure that Marco was just as well-endowed as his brother. The idea of all that hot, hard flesh filling her nearly had her eyes rolling back in her head.

*Sensory overload. They'll kill me if I don't regain some control. All I can think about is rolling around on them, under them.*

Rubio strutted across the short expanse of the bedroom to stand directly in front of her. She didn't think he'd taken his eyes off of her but that once. His intense stare had her nerve endings sizzling with something bigger than anticipation. When he reached out and touched her arm, Marco let go of that one so that Rubio could take one finger and rub it across the tip of his cock to gather up that drop of pre-cum. If she'd wondered what he meant to do with it, she wouldn't have long to wait. The devil of a cat lifted her hand and directed that finger to her lips.

"Taste what you do to me, *mi corazón*."

Taylor opened her mouth and presented the tip of her tongue. Rubio laid her finger on her tongue, and she closed her mouth to swirl it around the digit to get every molecule of taste off of it. Salty caramel with maybe a hint of pepper danced along her tongue. She swallowed and opened her eyes, not realizing that she'd closed them until then.

"Fuck!" Marco growled low in her ear. "That is so sexy, Taylor. I want to watch you do it again, but with my cum."

All she could do was whimper as a very nude and aroused Rubio pulled her into his arms, leaving Marco to undress this time. Instead of letting her watch Marco, he backed her up against the door and captured her mouth with his. True passionate lust overtook them both as he explored her mouth, rubbed along her tongue, and drank in her very breath.

Taylor gave as good as she accepted from him. Each suck or nibble she took one step further. The feel of his skin against hers ignited a burning need that only fucking would quench. She wasn't even sure if that would be enough. All she could think about was getting him inside of her. His angry dick pressed against her belly, more pre-cum leaking across her stomach as they moved against each other.

"Need. I need." She couldn't even complete the sentence.

"Yes. I know." Rubio grabbed her ass with both hands and lifted her so that she could wrap her legs around him.

"Yes!" It came out as a moaning hiss when he was able to align his cockhead with her wet, slick opening.

*One push. Just one push.*

"Rubio! Fuck me! I need you inside of me." Her voice came out shrill and demanding.

As if her words were all he needed in order to take her, Rubio pulled her down on his cock even as he thrust upward into her cunt. It took their breath. Neither of them moved for a full five seconds.

Taylor threw her head back, gasping in breath, and hit her head hard on the door. She wouldn't have even noticed if Marco hadn't cursed a blue streak at his brother.

"What the fuck? Get her away from the door." Marco's voice captured her attention long enough to notice that, though he was identical to Rubio in just about every way, his dick had a slight curve to it that his brother's didn't have.

"So hot, Marco. She'll burn you up. Hurry or we will miss our chance, brother." Rubio held Taylor, still completely full of his cock.

No matter how hard she squirmed, he didn't let her move an inch. He cooed soothing words in her ear, promising it would be so good if she could just hold on a bit longer. Taylor didn't care how it would feel later. She knew how she felt right then, and she needed him to move.

Before she'd even finished that thought, fingers probed her back hole and some type of lubricant was pressed into the passage. She'd hadn't played much with anal sex since, to most shifters, it was used more to show dominance than anything else. With her mates, it would be about the pleasure and not about power. She already knew that they were stronger than she was, but she also knew that she would hold a great deal of power over them as their mate.

Any additional thoughts she might have had vanished as a pair of thick fingers saturated with the lube breached her back entrance, coating the inside of her ass in the process of stretching her just this side of pain. By the time a third finger joined the other two, Taylor couldn't help pushing back against the thick digits.

"Damn, Taylor. You're on fire. I'll never manage to get inside that tight ass without blowing my load. Stop for me, *cariño*. Let me inside of you before it is too late for me." Marco's voice had squeezed down to biting words between clenched teeth, his words coming out in a lisp as his teeth took over his mouth.

She struggled to remain still, whimpering when he began to push his hard cock against her puckered hole. It burned—burned really good—until he finally breached the first muscular ring. Once he'd fully seated himself deep within her ass, Taylor realized that with both males inside her body, there wasn't room for her. She couldn't breathe, talk, or even swallow. Anything that required her to move in any way was just impossible with that much flesh filling her body.

Just when she thought she'd pass out from lack of oxygen, Marco pulled almost all the way out then pressed back inside of her while Rubio pulled out. The back and forth motion as the two brothers shared her between them soon had the previous fire that had tamped down for a while begin to smolder once more.

"Holy hell, man." Rubio's voice held a hoarse raspy sound where before it had been deep and smooth like rich chocolate. "Can't stand it much longer. She's got my dick in a vise and isn't letting go. I'm going to come if we don't either slow her down or speed us up."

"We can slow down next time," she snarled. "Move. Now!"

They moved, shifting her between them as one pulled out and the other worked their way in. The burning sting of Marco in her ass had become more and less all at the same time. Less pain but more pleasure. Less burn and more pressure.

Taylor couldn't tell where one started and the other left off. They were surrounding her, inside of her, and somewhere in between. She gave up fighting the slow rhythm they'd settled into and concentrated instead on reaching her climax. They would follow if she could catch that illusive sliver of light and hold on. The moment she did, the ride began.

It started at her toes, curling them until they cramped, then moved up her legs, her thighs until her belly felt as if she'd double over with the pressure. The pleasure built, pulling from every nerve ending until, finally, she perched on the cliff, waiting for that one last sensation that would throw her over into a free fall of pure, unrestrained pleasure.

"Fuck! Now, Marco."

Rubio's face contorted as his fingers dug into her ass and he thrust one last time, holding her there, his entire body going rigid as his climax attacked. It started a chain reaction with Taylor caught up in Rubio's release. The muscles in her ass and pussy contracted around Rubio's pulsing shaft. She swore that when the cat thrust up that last time he ground her clit against his pubic bone. It shattered her control if she'd had any left to begin with.

Her climax steamrolled over Marco as she clamped down around his dick, squeezing it until she felt every vein, bump, and curve. His swift intake of air was all the warning she had before hot cum filled her ass, sending another wave of explosions through her body. Rubio got his share of the reaction and all but collapsed back against the wall.

"Can't breathe!" Taylor was sure her lungs were going to explode.

The exertion of an earthquake of a climax and being stuffed by two thick cocks had her lungs losing the ability to expand.

"Marco? I can't move." Rubio's legs shook with the effort of standing with Taylor in his arms.

"Easy, *nene*. Let me take care of you." Marco was gentle as he pulled from her ass, helping to support her until his brother could pull from her dripping pussy.

"Can you stand, Taylor?" Rubio continued to hold the wall up, though his legs appeared less shaky now.

"Catch my breath." She had to work to slow her breathing down so that she made sense. "I can stand."

"Good. Let's take a shower and then get something light to eat before we go to bed." Marco eased her toward the other side of the room where the bathroom was situated.

"Did we just have a three-way?" she asked Marco when he'd set her on the vanity while he turned on the water for the shower.

He chuckled. "I believe we did. And it was a damn good one, too."

Taylor couldn't help but giggle like a young kitten with her first crush. When she'd been young, the idea of a ménage was too taboo to speak about. It was known to happen, but few females ever talked about them. Now she no longer had to wonder.

"What is that smirk for on your face, *cariño*? No secrets." Marco stepped over to where she sat on the cold marble of the double vanity. "Tell me."

"I was just thinking that now I'm one of those females who's had a ménage but won't tell any of the young girls about it. I can remember watching a friend's older sister prance around because she knew there were rumors that she'd had sex with a wolf shifter and a lynx shifter at the same time. She would never admit it or talk about it. Instead she just fed the rumors by winking at us younger females."

"Naughty sex stories. You're going to have to share more with us before we fall asleep."

"Share what before we fall asleep?" Rubio asked as he finally shuffled into the bathroom.

"Dirty little stories about when she was a young kit still wet behind her ears." Marco grinned down at her when she shot him a dirty look.

"Come on in with you. The water's hot, and there's enough steam to satisfy my grumpy brother."

"I'm not grumpy. I just like it to be hot when I soak." Rubio stepped out of the shower and into the massive tub then slowly sank into the water. His face relaxed as he closed his eyes and moaned his appreciation.

"You'd think he loves this bath more than he loved coming inside of you earlier," Marco snickered.

"Taylor, you know that isn't true. I'm just overly content after having made love to my mate and starting our quest for producing lots of little kits to spoil." Rubio opened one eye to glare across the tub at his brother.

She stiffened at Rubio's mention of conceiving. She didn't need any more pressure than what they already had to endure if she had any chance of becoming pregnant. Taylor cleared her throat.

"What is it, precious? I can feel the tension returning to your body. Your shoulders have tightened, and there is a slight tremor there." Marco pulled her back in a tighter embrace. "Talk to us. There can be no secrets between mates."

"I'm worried that I won't be able to get pregnant. What will we do if I'm sterile? Many of the females in my Leap are. It's another reason my uncle wanted to find a Felix to join groups. There needs to be new blood to support more births."

"And that's what you have with us, Taylor, new blood. Our shadow has been blessed with a high fertility rate since we opened our shadow to other shifters. Since, as you have pointed out, many jaguar males used to travel from shadow to shadow to court new females, there had been no shortage of fresh seed in our group." Rubio took her foot in his hands and began to rub it, applying pressure at key points that nearly put her into a trance it felt so good.

"Now that our males have begun to yearn for a permanent home with a mate and kits, the worry over a stagnant gene pool began to build with our Sire. It is another reason he was seeking a new home for us. New territory allowed for mating between our jaguars and other groups." Marco's mouth worried a spot just below her ear. He licked and nibbled so that she began to anticipate when he would change from one to the other.

"I pray you're right. The fact that I never conceived with my first mate…"

"What?" Rubio jerked back and stood up. "You've been mated before? Why haven't you told us this?"

## Chapter Eight

Taylor's surprise at his reaction failed to distract her from watching the water pour off of Rubio's hard muscles to run down his cut abs and tight thighs. Her mouth watered with need. She wanted to lick every drop from his body. She actually pulled from Marco's embrace and leaned toward his brother.

She snapped her eyes up to meet Rubio's glittering gold ones. Anger and betrayal shown in them and the tightness of his jaw.

"I'm sorry. I thought you knew. I guess I thought we talked about why I was so opposed to mating in the first place, but I guess we didn't get around to that discussion since we had to meet with Jag again." She looked between the two males. "I had no intention of ever mating again. I wasn't going to accept you two either, except ours turned out to be a true mating and my cat demanded I accept that."

"So you aren't accepting of us as your mates, but since your cat is, you feel you have to go along?" Rubio cursed in his language even as he climbed out of the tub and snatched a towel. Taylor recognized a word or two, and they weren't nice words.

"No! Stop twisting my words." She slapped the water with both hands then stood up as her anger finally overtook her. "I refused to accept another mate. I've perfected the ability to close off my feelings so that I don't fall prey to male hormones. My cat insisted I accept you, which made me relax around you. I realized then that we were true mates. It wasn't that I only accepted you because she insisted. She just insisted that I wake up and notice."

Taylor threw in a few expletives of her own as she stomped from the tub over to where the towels were. Rubio beat her to them and held one out for her. Even when angry and hurt, he treated her with respect. She couldn't remain angry with him for long when he shot down her grumpiness with his innate chivalrous nature.

"Rubio. The fact that she was and isn't now is all that matters. What I want to know is why she isn't anymore." Marco finally got out of the tub, as well.

"It is obvious, brother. He died leaving her without a mate and guardian. Her great-uncle took over that role."

Taylor sighed and walked out of the bathroom to find something to put on. "No, Rubio. That isn't the case. He's still very much alive. More's the pity, though."

The two males stalked after her, crowding her as she pulled on a sleeping shirt. She could sense their confusion. It was unheard of for a mated pair to separate for any reason other than death or finding one's true mate.

"He found his true mate and left you?" Marco asked.

"No. My great-uncle dissolved the mating. He should have banished the male but didn't. I have to see him almost daily. It upsets me knowing he's still around."

"Explain, Taylor." Rubio spat out the two words through his clenched jaw.

Taylor wanted to tell him to go jump in a lake or, better yet, fuck himself but knew he had a right to know. She should have told them earlier, but she honestly thought she'd told them about it.

"My father found out he had the feline cancer that we sometimes get. It worried him to leave me without a guardian, so he arranged a mating between me and a friend's son. I was upset by it but didn't want to cause my father more pain, so I agreed. When my father died, I took on my new mate and found that the choice hadn't been a good one. He had anger issues and took them out on me one time too many. I was finally able to convince my great-uncle to dissolve the mating due to cruelty. It took six months of enduring his beatings in order to gather enough evidence to prove that he was mistreating me." She sighed and tried to shut the door to that part of her life once more, but it proved stubborn. When Marco reached out to touch her, Taylor flinched away.

"Dammit, Taylor. You know I would never hurt you. Don't pull away from me now. Not after the joy we experienced only an hour ago."

Rubio stepped over to where she stood next to the bed and knelt in front of her. "I'm sorry, *cariño*. I lost my temper, and that's uncalled for with you. I don't know what is going on with me. Ever since I met you, my emotions have been all over the place. Please forgive me, my mate."

It took blinking her eyes several times and swallowing hard to keep hot tears from falling at his eloquent apology. The fact that he'd apologized at all spoke volumes. Males were normally too proud to ever admit they might be wrong. She'd not only accept his apology but treasure it.

"There is nothing to forgive, Rubio. I should have told you both sooner. It's something I've tried very hard to forget, so I didn't remember that it might be important. Will you forgive me?" Taylor cupped Rubio's face in her hands.

"It would have been better on all of us if you had, but I understand that you just didn't think about it. There is no need for your apology either, mate." Rubio stood, holding his hands over hers still pressed against his cheeks.

Taylor looked over Rubio's shoulder to see Marco's face relax as the tight lines that had formed when Rubio lost his temper slowly smoothed out. He nodded his head when he noticed that she was watching him. She lifted the corners of her mouth in a silent smile before returning her attention to his brother.

"Rubio. The hour is late. It's time to rest. Our poor mate is swaying on her feet. I'll tidy the bed. Why don't you fix her some hot cocoa while I do?" Marco rubbed one shoulder with his callused hand before dropping a soft kiss there.

"Come, sweetness. You will love my cocoa. I put a pinch of cinnamon in it and use real cream." Rubio guided her back down the hall to the kitchen. "Have a seat while I fix this."

Taylor allowed him to position her at the table so that they could see one another. She got the feeling that he needed to see her all the time since a threat to their mating. She wanted to be close to him, as well.

"I take two cups of cream and slowly warm it on a low temperature so as not to scald it. Once it begins to get a tiny ring of bubbles along the outer edge next to the sides of the boiler, I turn off the heat and add two tablespoons of dark cocoa, a dash of cinnamon, and a tablespoon of sugar." She watched him as he followed through with the steps.

"It smells delicious, Rubio." She felt her mouth water, and her leopard began to purr.

"Don't beat it, rather slowly stir it until everything is mixed to perfection." He poured the mouthwatering concoction into a mug and handed it to her. "Drink up while it's still warm."

She sipped the steaming drink and smiled as the delicious flavor of fresh cream and cocoa laced with a bite of sassy cinnamon awakened her taste buds. How had she not known about this? The packaged hot chocolate mixes she'd used in the past would never be enough for her again.

"Heaven, Rubio. I swear this is how heaven will be when I die." She took another sip, allowing the rich mixture to roll around in her mouth and tease her taste buds.

She watched the big feline grow a size taller under her praise. His chest swelled even as his eyes darkened. It seemed that she'd woken the jaguar from his slumber. As much as she'd love another romp, the human side of her was exhausted. She hadn't gotten a full nap in earlier. Taylor was operating through a ton of stress on less than six hours of sleep in the last twenty-four hours.

Rubio must have picked up on her weariness since he took the empty mug from her hand and swung her up into his arms with ease. He nuzzled her forehead as he walked from the kitchen, down the short hall, and pushed open the bedroom door with one foot.

"She's just about asleep on her feet, brother. Settle her in, and I'll be right back once I've cleaned up after the cocoa. I can't wait to snuggle with her all night. I'm not even sure I'll be able to sleep." Rubio handed her off to his brother.

"I take it she enjoyed your concoction." Marco turned with her and settled her onto the comfortable mattress. She moaned for him, snuggling deeper beneath the sheets.

"You could say that. I'm honestly not sure if she truly tasted it or just conked out and was too embarrassed to tell me."

"Not true. I tasted it, and it was very good. Don't you remember?" Taylor yawned, covering her mouth with one hand. "But I am sleepy. I'll just shut my eyes while I wait on the two of you."

Taylor heard their soft chuckles before she lost the fight to remain awake and drifted down a lazy river of dreams.

* * * *

"We need to consider our businesses, brother, and how we'll deal with them from the States. I think we should sell the medicinal plant business to Jorden. He's been exceptionally loyal to us and has worked as if it were his business ever since we hired him. Handling that type of business from such a distance would be nearly impossible. Timing is essential with it." Rubio spoke to him in a soft voice so as not to disturb their sleeping mate.

Marco nodded. "I agree. I can tell you're working under the assumption that we'll be moving to the States."

"I believe we will. I'm not sure in what capacity that will be, but we'll be moving. Did you notice how on edge Diaz appeared this second time we met with Jag? There's something more going on besides this mating issue with the Washington Felix." Rubio rinsed off the boiler then the mug.

"I still want to ask Taylor what she meant about something not being part of their agreement. I'm thinking it has nothing to do with this initial mating she was in or the actual appeal to our Felix for his assistance in securing a leader for his Leap."

"We'll ask her in the morning. Right now she needs sleep more than she needs another interrogation by either of us. We've got to cement our relationship with her before we even attempt to work on the other issues at hand." Rubio dried the boiler before picking up the mug and putting it away.

"I agree. I'm not sure how we can do that, but we need to figure it out sooner rather than later." Marco walked across the room to peek through the door and down the hall to where their bedroom door remained firmly closed. "Taylor will have to be treated equally with us. She's headstrong and independent to a fault. Any attempt we make at clipping her wings will damage our worthiness in her eyes."

"I have no problem seeing her in that light. She's intelligent and isn't afraid to speak her mind." Rubio closed his eyes, and an image of her giving him a verbal tongue-lashing while riding his cock sent a wave of need coursing through his bloodstream.

"I don't even want to know what you're thinking about over there." Marco's amused voice interrupted a very satisfying daydream.

"Create your own wet dream, brother. I'm not sharing mine." Rubio snickered when the dishtowel his brother had aimed at him fell short of its mark. He grabbed at it and jerked it from his brother's hands.

"What of the transportation boats? Those won't handle well from abroad either. Even if we found someone we trusted, by the time news reached us of any problems, it would be too late to fix them."

"You're right. It's possible one of the pilots will want to buy out the boats from us. The remainder of our businesses are easily handled from anywhere in the world. It will take some time, but it's doable.

Securing our passage to the US will take time for visas and all the other paperwork that goes along with moving from one country to the next."

Marco jerked his chin in the direction of their sleeping mate. "I'm ready to curl up with Taylor now. We can put our plans into action first thing in the morning. Nothing can be accomplished tonight."

"I'm going to scribble a few notes so we don't forget what we've decided. I also want to start a list of things we need to talk about tomorrow. Taylor will need to be involved in most of them." Rubio shoved his brother toward the doorway leading to the hall. "Go on and keep our mate company. I'll be along in a few minutes."

Marco didn't have to be told twice. He folded the dishtowel he'd caught when Rubio had tried to pop him back with it earlier. Leaving it on the counter, his twin stalked toward their bedroom with mischief dancing merry in his eyes.

He could imagine what his brother might be up to and hated that he might miss out on all the fun, but planning for their future took precedence for the moment. Moving from one side of the rain forest to the other took major planning, but moving the entire household across a country's border would be an entirely different challenge.

Where before they had only their own preferences and needs to accommodate, now they had a mate's wishes and requirements to consider in the equation. Hers would even take precedence over theirs as long as they didn't involve her safety or well-being.

*I will make it my priority in the mating to make sure she has everything she needs and never has to worry about anything. She will come to trust us once she sees that we are serious when we tell her we will be loyal to her and any kits we're blessed with. I have no wish to ever look at another female with our mate standing in front of us.*

She'd hurt his pride when she'd questioned his intentions. That she had every right to do so and a lot of reasons to wonder hadn't helped at the time. Now, as he stood back and thought about Jaguar history, he could see her concerns. It was only recently that males no longer wished to roam, spreading their seed and their affections with almost any willing female. Instead, they'd begun to settle down with one shadow and help raise the kits.

He wondered what had changed with their species. Neither he nor his brother had ever felt the urge to roam. Almost from the moment they'd discovered the joys of a female's body they'd planned to find their mate and make a home with her and their offspring. There'd never been any question between them.

Rubio vowed right then to make sure their young knew the value of a secure home with both a female and a male or two as role models. Their sons would treat females with respect to be protected, cared for, and even spoiled to some extent. Though their *padre* hadn't been around, their *madre* had drilled it into them as young cubs to always respect a female and that mating meant creating a home with both parents, not just a *madre* as they'd had. She'd drilled it into them that it was their responsibility to provide that home for their mate and cubs.

It was a lesson he and Marco had never forgotten. He only wished their *madre* could have met Taylor and known that they were fulfilling her wishes for them. Rubio finished the lists and looked up toward the ceiling.

"We will honor your teaching, Madre. We are making a home with our mate."

# Chapter Nine

Taylor stretched from her toes all the way up her legs, her back, and up her arms as she reached high above her head. It felt good to finally be standing on two feet without a pair of rutting males nosing her all over. She grinned despite how tender she was in places. They'd definitely worked hard to provide her everything she might need in order to conceive.

When they weren't busy screwing like rabbits all over the bedroom, Rubio was plying her with food and reading from one of his many lists for her approval. Marco kept Rubio from organizing them to death and provided the meat for the meals his brother cooked for her.

They'd waited for three days to hear from the shadow's Felix on what his answer would be to her great-uncle. Three days with no word or hint of his plans had them antsy and a little worried. It had been Marco who suggested a run. Taylor was onboard with that idea. The males were eager to introduce her to their world and her leopardess tugged on Taylor's control.

Right now, the two jaguars were out making sure there was nothing too dangerous in the area where they would run. Marco scouted farther out while Rubio remained close to her in case she needed him.

*As if. I've been taking care of myself since I was twelve. Someone had to when Papa began to shut down. I can hold my own in any fight or attack. I've had to be able to since there was no one I trusted enough to watch my back.*

That ended now. She had not one devoted mate, but two. She wouldn't have to always watch over her shoulder for threats. Her mates would share the burden of keeping guard. The relief that flooded her soul when she finally realized that nearly sent her to her knees.

"Taylor! *Cariño*." Rubio's husky voice always gave her goosebumps.

"In here. I just finished dressing." She strode toward the door, but Rubio threw it open before she made it there.

"Whoa. Where's the fire, Romeo?"

He stopped and stared down at her as if she'd lost her mind. "What fire? There's no fire."

Taylor burst out laughing even as she wrapped her arms around his waist. "That's the whole point. You're racing around as if something's on fire that you need to put out. Slow down, mate. I'm not going anywhere."

"I'm excited to show you our home. Marco is ready, and I can't wait to introduce you to some of our nature friends. They all know us in our jaguar form, so don't be disappointed if they refuse to allow you close at first. We appreciate your uniqueness, but some of them will need a little time." Rubio wagged his brows up and down as his dark eyes grew thick with emotion.

"Let's go! I've needed this for nearly a week now."

Taylor followed Rubio through the house and out the French doors leading from the living room out onto a covered veranda of sorts. Marc remained in his shifted state, a work of art displayed before her. His shiny black coat held a hint of palm-sized rosettes beginning low on his sides and circling beneath his belly. The sun sifting through the canopy overhead sprinkled shards of golden light that almost reflected off his rich black coat.

"Wow! You're gorgeous, Marco." She turned to stare up into Rubio's eyes. "Change for me. I want to see you both with my human eyes first."

Rubio grinned, and then the corners of his mouth turned up in a smirk. "You know Marco is going to make you pay for calling him gorgeous. We're males. We're handsome or amazing or viral. We aren't girly names."

"I calls 'em as I sees 'em, Romeo. Now strip!" She stepped back as Rubio shucked his clothes in seconds then flowed into his cat.

She'd never seen anything that sensuous before in her Leap. No one she knew was able to transform that quickly and with so much grace. Rubio's shift had progressed in one fluid movement that didn't even appear to hurt.

*How did he do that? I wonder if Marco can do that, as well. I hope they can teach me to shift like that. A-fucking-mazing!*

"Wow. Just, wow."

She stared at the two sleek but muscular cats, their mouths slightly open as they took in as much of her scent as they could through their nose as well as their oral cavities. Saliva dripped from their massive teeth, but neither of them posed the least bit of danger to her. She was their fated mate. They'd kill for her and die if it were necessary. She prayed that never became a question in their lives.

Marco took a step forward and lifted his head and chuffed at her. It was obvious he was anxious for her to change, as well. She smiled, crossed her arms to grasp the hem of her shirt, and pulled it over her head to drop it at her feet. Then she removed the shorts she'd just put on and progressed to her bra and panties.

"Look, guys. I can't change like you to do. You make it look so easy, like pouring water from a pitcher over some round rocks. I can't compete with that."

Rubio padded over to nudge her at the hip. He whined and nudged her again. It was obvious he was just as impatient as his brother.

"Okay, okay." Taylor knew this change would be a little harder than normal because she hadn't been able to shift in nearly a week now.

As she pictured her leopardess in her mind, she relaxed her muscles and breathed out as the cat inside of her ran up her body to pour out until she'd taken over her human side completely. It sounded just as if hers had been just as fluid and serene as the twins', but in reality, it hurt—a lot since it had been so long between her shifts. She could also tell it had been jerky instead of the smooth transition the males had exhibited.

The two jaguars pushed against her from either side. Rubbing their heads up and down her body, back and forth around her neck and at her tail end. Her leopardess snapped at Rubio when he shoved his nose where it didn't belong. Marco made a huffing noise that sounded like a laugh to her.

She was tired of sniffing and took the lead when she suddenly broke out into a run. Where the jaguars could easily keep up with her for short distances, they would tire faster than she would due to their size. She had more endurance since she was smaller, less bulky, and because she had a better lung capacity to work with.

Some other differences were in their coats. Where she had lovely rosettes, as well, theirs had small circles in the middle of them. Her tail was longer than theirs, and her muzzle was a little longer than their more compact head housing massive and powerful jaws that could crack a skull.

As she raced through the jungle, Marco nudged her shoulder to turn her in a different direction. Rubio remained on her other side, keeping her between them as they raced through the foliage, easily jumping over logs and avoiding thick vines.

A whiff of something exotic and mouth watering curled in her nose.

*Prey.*

She chuffed and slowed to get the general direction of the wind and the location of potential food. The two males slowed with her and lifted their noses, as well. Marco nodded his head and sent a guttural clicking noise her way. He was on board with a hunt. The only question she had now was if they would allow her to take it down.

*Mine. Kill.*

She lowered her head and stalked around to ease up down wind of their prey. Dinner proved to be a tapir. She'd never had one before but instinctively knew it would be good to eat. She hunkered down to the ground to get an idea of where everything was around her and waited for the animal to turn in the opposite direction to give her time to sneak up. She could sense the two jaguars hanging back to let her have the fun.

She silently eased closer and closer to the animal until she was able to make a short dash and catch the animal unawares. One powerful bite to the tapir's neck and the snap of his neck was sweet music to her ears. A clean kill was always welcome. She stood over her meal and sang out her triumph to her two mates. Then, as they loped toward her, she grinned and snatched up her dinner and dragged it across to a tree before she carted up to drape it over a branch and began eating.

The look of confusion and amazement by the two males below her was well worth the verbal lashing she might get later for not sharing. She'd share, but only after she'd gotten her fill. It was, after all, her kill.

The two males huffed and chucked at her then stretched out to wait for her to finish. She could get to like living here if that became necessary. The hunting was much more fun and interesting.

*But I'd miss my friends. And I'd worry about what happened to them if the Felix decides not to accept the offer.*

That quickly killed her appetite after only a few good bites of the tasty meat. She nosed the meat over the limb so it fell just inches from poor Rubio's nose. He hissed at her but quickly pulled the remains over so that Marco could share with him. He looked up as if expecting her to join them on the jungle floor, but she liked the vantage point she held in the tree. She'd wait on them to finish eating then follow them.

Their world was so different from hers. How would they react to living in Washington? The forests there were a little like the jungle here but with different types of vegetation, but there wasn't near the selection of prey there. Would the hassle of relocating and possibly needing to fight other challengers outweigh whatever issues they had here? She knew that the cartels were a problem, but she didn't know much more than that. They'd mostly kept their problems to themselves.

What would she do if they ended up staying here or even moving to the New England states? She didn't think they'd like the winters there, but if the situation here was dire enough, they might seriously consider it. Could she leave everything she knew to be with them?

*They're our true mates, cat. I don't want to live without them.*

Only time would tell. She didn't even want to think about what would happen if she didn't conceive. There was no way she'd mate Jag. It would break her, and she was sure the twins would want to challenge their Felix. That would break them. Why did her great-uncle have to play with other people's lives like he did?

A rather irritated roar jerked her awake to stare down at the two males. Dinner was completely gone. Though she could still smell the slightest scent of the meat, she couldn't see it anywhere. Where had they stashed it?

Again a chuff as Marco advanced to the trunk of the tree, a very real threat that he'd come up and get her if she didn't hurry down. Taylor couldn't help but smile inside as the leopardess calmly swiped her tongue over her paws before climbing to the bottom limb and jumping down. She strolled at a leisurely pace over to where Rubio stood with a snarl curling his lips and showing a bit of his sharp smile.

They turned her in a new direction and padded at a brisk pace just short of a run until they reached a deep stream. Both males splashed in and swam around, ducking their head and shaking the water off when they emerged. When she didn't follow them, Marco swam over and stepped up on the bank. He tried to nuzzle her into the stream, but she was having none of it.

Didn't they know that leopards didn't like water? Her leopardess was an excellent swimmer but didn't enjoy getting wet one bit. This they would have to enjoy without her. She backed up a few paces and stretched out in a spotlight of sunshine while the two overly large pups played and splashed around.

The next thing she knew, the jaguars were nudging her once more. It was growing dark and time to return to their home. Though both leopards and jaguars hunted at dusk and just before dawn, their human halves needed to return to reality.

They romped on the way back, pushing and shoving each other as they play-fought for dominance. Naturally the males won but not without a little run for the title. When they walked back up on the veranda, the two jaguars changed first to get a human look at their mate in her leopard form.

"You're so beautiful, *cariño*." Rubio rubbed down her neck and scratched behind her ears.

"Amazing. Look at those gorgeous colors. Unlike our black, you have flames in your coat. The rosettes are perfectly formed and make you look like a cat to be feared and respected." Marco touched his forehead to hers before rubbing his mouth all along the side of hers, scent marking them both and mixing their individual essences much like they would soon be once the mating ritual was completed. They would exchange bites, thus mixing their blood once their Felix had everything settled with her Felix. If it took too long, he wasn't waiting.

"Come on back, *mi amor*." Marco stepped back, pulling Rubio with him.

Taylor hated this part, but maybe over time, they could teach her their trick for making the shift so much easier. She couldn't help but wonder as she pictured herself in human form and began breathing in and out to initiate the change if all of the jaguars changed that effortlessly. She'd have to ask them.

Her bones creaked as her skin absorbed the spotted fur of her leopardess. It hurt and burned, but she refused to cry out from the pain. She wouldn't go so long without shifting again.

By the time she'd returned to her human form, she was tired and shaky. The twins wrapped a towel around her, and Rubio picked her up, concern on his face as he carried her into the house.

"*Mi tesoro*. Why does it hurt you so? I've never seen one fight it so hard as you seem to." Rubio rubbed his chin on top of her head before he laid her gently on the bed and followed her down.

"I don't fight it. It's just how I change, though normally it isn't quite that bad. I haven't shifted in nearly a week. I do better when I can shift at least every other day." Her voice wobbled a bit but grew steadier the more she talked.

"To us it looks as if you fight your leopardess for control. Does she resist letting you emerge?" Marco joined them on the bed.

Where she had the large towel wrapped around her, the twins lounged next to her in all their naked glory. Even as exhausted as she was, Taylor couldn't help but admire their bodies. Even in a relaxed state, their cocks lay long and heavy over their thighs. If she licked her lips, it wasn't on purpose.

Groans told her she'd aroused them even before their dicks began to rise for attention. She'd be more than happy to taste and lick them if they'd only let her.

"Don't, Taylor. You are in no condition for lovemaking right now. Rest and we promise to satisfy you later." Rubio kissed her cheek and opened her towel so that he could wrap one arm around her waist.

"You won't let me taste you." She knew her mouth formed a pout since she'd tried for the look.

"Careful, kitten. Don't try to sway us. We won't waste one drop of our seed until you're carrying our cubs. Then you can devour us to your heart's desire," Marco promised.

"Just let me lick them. That won't waste anything." She knew she was being childish, but really. "One lick each?"

"Once that velvet mouth of yours and that tempting tongue touches our dicks we'd be lost and helpless to stop you from going any further. No, we are steadfast in this, *mi amor*. Patience."

\* \* \* \*

A warm tongue swiped across her shoulder as she slowly opened her eyes to find Rubio straddling her waist and licking up her neck and across her shoulder. The long leisurely laps of his tongue elicited shivers along her spine and goosebumps along her arms.

"There you are. I thought you might sleep the night away."

"I had a great run earlier and a good meal. That's about all it takes to put me to sleep." She stretched beneath him. The heat from his hard cock rubbed against her belly. "Looks like someone is up and ready to play."

His eyes flashed with humor as his mouth curved into a smirk. She wiggled her hips against the bed, grinding her pelvis against his thick cock in the process.

"Careful, little one. You'll start something we don't have time to finish. Marco will be very miffed at us if we have a quick romp when we're supposed to be getting ready."

"Ready for what?" Taylor drew her brows together as a sliver of unease replaced the earlier shivers down her spine.

Rubio sighed. "Jag is ready to tell us his decision. We need to get ready. I knew you'd want to shower first so I woke you a little early. Marco wasn't happy with me, but he realized that it would be wise."

Taylor's sliver of unease turned into full-blown frogs bouncing around in her gut. This was it. They'd find out what their future would be, and she, Marco, and Rubio would have to make some serious decisions. While she'd been anxious to get it over with, part of her wished for more time.

"Move off me, Rubio. I've got to shower and figure out something to wear. I don't have anything suitable to wear. This is ridiculous. Had I known I would be here more than a night or two at the most, I would have packed more clothes. It's all the Felix's fault." She scooted out from under him when he merely lifted off of her but remained in place.

"Which Felix, kitten?"

"Don't get smart with me, water cat. How can your jaguar enjoy swimming and playing in the water? That's just wrong. Cats don't like water." She stomped into the bathroom and turned on the shower to let the water warm. "Now my human side, she loves water and swimming."

"That doesn't make sense, *cariño*. You are your leopardess as well as human. How can one like something and the other not?" he asked from the other room.

"I don't think we are as connected to our cats as you guys are here. You seem to think as one. We tend to think independently of each other."

She stepped into the spray of the shower and moaned in pleasure as the water washed away her shift and lazy dozing. Remembering why she was in the shower in the first place, Taylor washed as quickly as possible while still being thorough. As much as she wanted to drag her feet, it wouldn't change whatever decision the Felix had reached.

Rubio stood with a towel held out wide for her to step into when she got out of the shower. He dried her off and helped her comb out her wild mass of curls, laughing when she cursed him over an especially stubborn knot.

"Just wait until you get that long ponytail in a knot. I'll show you how it feels."

He lifted his chin, giving her an arrogant smile complete with lifted brows. "I never get knots or tangles in my hair. We must teach you how to keep your hair under control."

Taylor met his eyes that appeared so serious and frowned at him. She quickly turned around and poked him in the ribs.

"Don't get all haughty with me, *gato*."

When he pounced, Taylor managed to slip beneath his arm and run away. She grabbed her case and began rummaging through it for the only other outfit she had. Pulling it out, she groaned. It needed pressing and was by no means suitable for an occasion such as this. Their lives literally hung in the balance. Either they would pick up and move to Washington State or they would possibly move to the New England states.

*Or we could stay here. I wouldn't mind that like I thought I would. Yes, I'd miss my friends, but I will make new ones here and have my mates without the worry of needing to get pregnant right away.*

"Stop it, Taylor. You're going to wring the poor blouse to death." Rubio pulled the rumpled mess from her fingers and ticked his tongue as he tossed it to the bed. "We had a friend bring you something to wear. She is close to your size, and we think it will look wonderful on you."

Red-hot rage prickled her eyes as a growl escaped her throat. Her leopardess lifted her head, and the hair at the back of her neck lifted.

"Taylor? What is it?" Rubio actually took a step back.

"You would ask an ex-lover to bring something for me to wear and expect me to put it on?" She stalked toward him, her claws escaping her fingers at her side.

"Easy, sweet kitten. We never played with Serisa. She is mated and one of our cousins. I swear to you we would never even think of such a thing. You will like Serisa, I promise." Rubio backed up another step with his hands lifted in front of him.

She stopped, and the blinding haze slowly dissipated, leaving her embarrassed and a bit ashamed, as well. She'd never acted like this before. What was wrong with her?

*I'm jealous of my mates. I'd kill any female that even approaches them. I have got to get control of it, or I'll end up hurting someone by accident.*

"I'm sorry, Rubio. I don't know why I jumped like that. My leopardess was ready to rend some poor female end from end. This could be a problem." She was sure it would be a problem.

"It won't be this bad once we've completed the mating. We still have time for you to conceive. Even if Jag plans to accept your Felix's proposition, it will take time to make arrangements to move an entire shadow. Housing will need to be secured for us, and we will need to apply for visas."

He walked over to the closet and pulled out a lovely dress that looked to have been hand made with a multitude of colors. When she pulled it on, it both caressed her body and floated out around it when she moved.

"Wow. It almost feels alive. Look how it moves when I move."

Rubio smiled, but it was a predatory smile with teeth. "Yes. It looks amazing on you. I'm picturing taking it off when we return home."

She sighed and rolled her eyes. "We better hurry. I bet Marco is about to have a cow as long as it's taken for me to get ready."

"Actually you've dressed much faster than I thought possible for a female." Marco walked into the room and reached out to take her hand, twirling her around to get a better look at her. "Magnificent. Serisa knew just what to send."

"Careful, brother. I nearly ended up castrated for mentioning another woman's name." Rubio's mouth curved up in a cat-got-the-canary smile.

Marco's eyes went wide even as his brows lifted. "I didn't think of that. I'm so sorry, *cariño*. We should have explained before we ever asked her to borrow a dress."

"It's not me you should tell you're sorry. Your brother is the one who bore the brunt of my ire. He managed to escape unscathed though." Taylor grinned at the male who'd nearly lost his balls.

"My apologies, Marco. I'll let you remove the dress tonight while I watch."

"Let? What makes either of you think that I'll let either of you remove the dress?" She nearly burst out laughing at their chastised expressions.

For big bad jaguars, they were so kitty whipped. She was excited to be the one to snap them in line. The only thing that would make things perfect would be if she were to conceive before they left for the States.

"Come, my leopardess. We need to leave now. We don't want to keep the Felix waiting considering what is at stake here. My jaguar is pacing inside of me, and the thought that someone could take you from us has him on edge and ready to pounce. Please, please don't allow any other male close to you, *cariño*." Marco held out one arm for her to take.

Rubio followed them from the room and opened the door for them as they stepped out into the night to meet their destiny.

## Chapter Ten

"So good of you to join us."

Diaz's snide comment rankled Taylor's leopardess. She wanted to lash out but knew better for two reasons. One, he was the Felix's counsel, and two, her mates would annihilate him and be punished, maybe even exiled.

"Diaz. That's enough." Jag stood up from behind the desk and waited until Taylor sat down.

"I've reached a decision. Since it involves the three of you, I'm telling you before I announce it to the shadow." Jag resumed his seat. "I have decided to accept the Washington Felix's offer. I don't want Taylor as a mate and have made it more than clear to your Felix. He said that he would agree provided she conceives with the two of you prior to our arrival. If, at that time, she has not conceived, then we will face that should it be necessary."

"My Felix agreed to this?" Taylor couldn't believe he'd gone back on a decision he'd made. One of his greatest faults was the inability to change his mind, equating that to losing face.

"Not exactly," Jag said with a small smile that though it reached his eyes, it didn't take over his face.

"What does that mean?" Rubio asked.

Taylor could hear the growl in his voice. She reached up to squeeze the hand he'd laid on her shoulder.

"It means that I agreed to his proposal provided it agrees with my plans. I'm hoping that we won't have to worry about it when the time comes to travel to the US. But," he began, "if we do have that to overcome, we will decide on another course of action."

"Would you fight my great-uncle if it became necessary?" she asked.

"If it became necessary I would fight him, but I would spare his life and exile him. It would be the only way to maintain the leadership of your Leap. That way I hope your young males won't feel honor bound to defend him. I don't want to lose anyone to this." Jag lifted his chin in Marco's direction. "What is it, Marco? I can see the question or uncertainty in your face."

"It all seems too easy. I can't believe it will be that cut and dried. Nothing ever is."

"I agree," Rubio added.

The Felix sighed. "One wrench that could fuck up the plan is if we have to deal with the Leo of the Pride as soon as we arrive. More than likely he will plan to fight your Felix and win before I'm able to save him. I will remove the Leo myself, but if he gets wind that we are coming, he may well strike."

"That's what I'm afraid of. If that happens, there will be few of my Leap left for you to take over." Taylor's voice barely came out in a whisper. She'd known this was a possibility even before she knew about her great-uncle's plan to offer her as a token to seal their agreement.

"We will keep this as quiet as possible, but visa applications and plane manifests are public records, and anyone can monitor them." This came from Diaz. "I will make as few inquiries as is necessary to prepare everything for us to move."

Taylor squeezed Rubio's hand. "I appreciate that, Diaz."

Marco squeezed her shoulder. Was it in warning not to address the other cat or in approval that she'd acknowledged his plans for stealth? She would need to learn their moods before someone got hurt.

"I take it you have been busy these last three days while I've been making decisions that would affect all of us." Jag's elevated brows spoke of humor, but Taylor wasn't sure how to take the statement.

"With what is on the line, it's in our best interest to make every effort to secure Taylor as our mate." Marco took a step up so that he was just a little in front of her.

"Ease back, Marco. I'm not challenging you for her. I was making an observation." He got up and walked around the desk. "With your permission?" He lifted his hand toward Taylor.

The two males looked at each other and, after letting out long breaths, nodded. Taylor had no idea what they were agreeing to. She wasn't sure she liked it.

Jag took several steps closer to her then bent over and sniffed on either side of her neck. At the warning growls of her mates, he smiled at her and winked then stood up and eased back a few steps.

"Your scents are mingling already. It's amazing. Even without the mating ritual being completed you are already developing your mated scent." Jag grinned and nodded at Diaz to leave.

After the other male had closed the doors behind him, Jag leaned back against the front of his desk, looking cool and calm despite the enormity of the pressure on him.

"That's a good thing. It will support our case when the time comes to travel to the States," Marco told him.

"Indeed." Jag laced his fingers together and just stared at them for a few seconds. "I hadn't realized it would be true since the need has never come up before."

"Realize what was true?" Marco looked over at Rubio.

They both looked confused, and hell, she was confused. What was Jag talking about?

"That a Felix can sense certain things about his shadow before anyone else could know. Such as males always know when a female is ovulating. It is one of the ways we have been able to procreate throughout history." Jag didn't say anything else.

"Well?" Rubio asked with impatience, turning his brows down and his eyes narrow.

"Well, I can tell something that you, Taylor's mates, can't seem to tell yet." Jag's face split into a wide grin that had her a little nervous.

"What do you mean? We know she's ovulating. Why do you think we've been fucking every second we're awake?" Rubio demanded.

"Rubio!" She couldn't believe he'd be so crass as to blurt that out to their Felix of all males.

"Sorry. I don't get this game he's playing with us." Rubio leaned closer to her as he spoke. Marco remained slightly in front of her.

"A Felix of a Shadow or Leap, as far as I know, can always tell when a female has conceived before anyone else, including her mates." Jag just stood there watching them.

Taylor was the first to get what he'd said. She waited for the twins to catch on. The only warning she had was when Rubio grabbed her out of the chair and swung her around until Marco stopped him, reminding him she was pregnant.

"I can't believe you waited to tell us!" Marco scolded his Felix.

Jag just grinned wider. "It was fun to, for once, have good news to share. I wanted to savor it."

"Good news? No, this is great news, wonderful news." Rubio kissed her until she couldn't breathe.

Marco pulled him away and tugged her into his arms, hugging her and kissing her with just as much exuberance as his brother had. When Jag grabbed her next and gave her a warm hug but planted his kiss on the top of her head, everyone froze.

"Ah, hell. Just this once you can hug her without me ripping your throat out." Marco took her hand to bring her back into his and Rubio's arms. "Just don't think you can do it again."

Jag smiled. This time with a hint of teeth. "Wouldn't dream of it."

"We've got plans to make, mate. It will take at least three weeks or more to ready everything for us to travel there. You can stay in bed or the couch while we handle the details."

Jag drew in a breath through his teeth and retreated around to the back side of his desk.

"Excuse me? I can stay in bed? I'll do no such thing. I will be helping you make decisions and packing and planning our future. You will not banish me to a bed or a couch. We need to get this understood right here and right now." Taylor could see Jag fighting to keep from laughing as she chastised her mates.

Rubio and Marco looked at each other with open mouths. They turned as a unit to their Felix. When Marco started to speak, Jag cut him off with raised hands.

"I'm not in the middle of this, guys. This is your future, and you best think before you speak from this day forward."

"Or by death you will depart." Taylor finished for the Felix. "So, what is this about plans to make?"

# THE END

**WWW.MARLAMONROE.COM**

Siren Publishing, Inc.
www.SirenPublishing.com

Lightning Source UK Ltd.
Milton Keynes UK
UKHW02f1445070318
319039UK00006B/934/P